# ROUGH JUSTICE

ADAM CROFT

GET MORE OF MY BOOKS FREE!

To say thank you for buying this book, I'd like to invite you to my exclusive *VIP Club*, and give you some of my books and short stories for FREE.

To join the club, head to adamcroft.net/vip-club and two free books will be sent to you straight away! And the best thing is it won't cost you a penny — ever.

*Adam Croft*

For more information, visit my website: adamcroft.net

# BOOKS IN THIS SERIES

Books in the Knight and Culverhouse series so far:
1. Too Close for Comfort
2. Guilty as Sin
3. Jack Be Nimble
4. Rough Justice

To find out more about this series and others, please head to adamcroft.net/list.

1

Jeff Brelsford poured the last dregs of the coffee from the jug and switched off the hot-plate. The dark liquid steamed from his mug as the bitter aroma assaulted his nostrils.

It was late for coffee, but Jeff wasn't on Greenwich Mean Time with the rest of Mildenheath; he was running on Pacific Time. His contacts on the California coast would just be finishing their late breakfast or lunch and logging on to the forum.

The adrenaline surged in Jeff's chest every time he sat down at his laptop, opened TorBrowser and waited for the status bar to tell him the connection to the Tor network had been made and that he was completely protected and cloaked in anonymity.

The Dark Web was where Jeff had been spending

most of his time recently. It was a safe haven where he was able to find like-minded people who truly understood how it felt to be like him. He didn't think he was a bad man. He hadn't harmed anyone. Not directly, anyway.

It was a confusing place to be, inside a mind conflicted between a burning desire and a sense of injustice at what he saw to be a lack of understanding, stacked up against the knowledge that the rest of the world saw his predilections as vile and despicable. Deep down, he knew they were right. Underneath it all he knew his desires, although under control for now, could easily become dangerous.

He also knew he couldn't let that happen. He'd already been satisfying his desires to a degree that worried him, even though he was under the relative anonymity of the Dark Web.

By its very nature, the Dark Web was almost completely anonymous. An area of the internet based on hidden protocols, invisible to search engines and general users, the Dark Web was accessible only using the TorBrowser software. It had become home to enormous online drug markets, with websites such as Silk Road openly and brazenly offering illicit narcotics for sale, safe in the knowledge that the very structure of the Dark Web made it very difficult for anyone to find out who ran the sites or who their customers were.

The common currency of the Dark Web, Bitcoin,

allowed users to exchange money under the radar without linking it to their bank account or personal identity. In short, anything could be bought on the Dark Web, whether it be guns, fraudulently obtained credit card details or even hired assassins. Compared to that, Jeff had managed to convince himself that looking at photographs of young girls was relatively innocuous.

The forum had been set up a few months previously, unlisted on any Dark Web directories in order to ensure that only those who knew about it and had been personally invited would be able to access it. Jeff had been invited by a member of another forum, Deepest Desires, of which he'd been a member for a couple of years. Being invited to be part of the new, unnamed, forum had left Jeff feeling like the privileged new member of a secret club, heightening the surge of adrenaline he got every time he accessed it.

As Jeff saw it, it was far better that he and the other members of the forum got their kicks sharing pictures and titillating comments than actually going out and acting on their desires. That had got him into trouble before, and he couldn't go making that mistake again.

He gulped down two mouthfuls of the bitter coffee and licked his lips, catching the rogue droplets before they splashed onto the desk in front of him.

The laptop lid was barely open when the doorbell

rang, the harsh, shrill ringing catching him unawares and giving him a sudden start. He wasn't expecting visitors. He reasoned it was probably someone collecting for charity or trying to sell double-glazing, knocking on doors in the evening assuming that they'd be able to catch people at home.

He unlatched the door and pulled it open. The man who stood on the other side of the door was certainly not who he'd expected.

'Jeff Brelsford?' the man said, his hands pushed into the trouser pockets of his dark suit as he cocked his head sideways.

'Yeah, why?' Jeff replied, sensing that something wasn't quite right.

'I'm Detective Inspector Richard Thomson. Can I come in?'

Jeff faltered for a moment. Had he somehow dropped a bollock on the Dark Web and managed to allow the police to track him down? No, it wasn't possible.

Then again, it could be to do with the double-yellows he'd parked on a couple of weeks back. It had only been for a couple of minutes and he hadn't been given a ticket. Or had he? Had it blown off the windscreen and been logged on a system somewhere that he'd ignored it? No, they wouldn't get CID involved with something like that.

'Uh, have you got any ID?' Jeff asked, stalling for time.

'Certainly,' the man replied, taking his hands out of his trouser pockets and going to his inside jacket pocket.

Before Jeff could realise what the black and yellow unit in the man's hand was, his entire body went rigid and he lost all motor skills as twelve-hundred volts seared through his testicles.

## 2

Jeff knew a Taser wouldn't directly cause you to lose consciousness and assumed he must have hit his head when he fell. It was a strangely lucid thought to have on regaining consciousness, and he assumed it was his brain's way of trying to avoid coming to terms with the fact that there was a man stood over him with a huge pair of gardening shears.

It was the same man who'd Tasered him at his front door — he knew it was — although he couldn't make out the man's face behind the plastic body suit he was wearing.

He must've been out for some time, as not only had the man managed to put on a full plastic body suit, he'd also stripped Jeff naked and bound his hands and feet.

The man's voice came muffled and deep.

'I know who you are, Jeff Brelsford. Scum. Paedo scum. Do you know who I am?'

'No,' Jeff replied, shocked at how groggy his own voice sounded. 'But I'm presuming you're not a policeman.'

'Bright lad. Although not quite bright enough to have kept off my radar.'

'Who are you?' Jeff asked, now beginning to panic.

The man ignored him and pointed his shears at Jeff's crotch. 'How's it feeling down there now?'

'Sore.'

'Shame. Never mind. I'm sure the pain won't last long. In fact, I'm sure it won't. You should think yourself very lucky. Not as lucky as the rest of the world, though, being rid of paedo scum like you,' the man sneered in his face.

'What do you want?' Jeff croaked, growing increasingly desperate.

'Justice. Simple as that. Pure justice.'

'For what? I haven't done anything. Who are you?'

The man laughed confidently. 'You haven't done anything? Really? I think we both know what you've done. What you are.'

'I don't know what you mean,' Jeff replied.

'Oh, I think you do,' the man said, leaning in close to Jeff's face. 'The Dark Web. The forum.'

Jeff hoped to God that the man hadn't seen the glint of recognition in his eyes, but he knew the involuntary reaction must have shown. Before he could respond, a globule of saliva landed on his right eyeball.

'You're scum. Nothing more, nothing less. Do you

understand that?' the man said as Jeff tried in vain to lift his tied arm to wipe his eye. Instead, all he could do was to wipe it with his shoulder the best he could.

'I'm sorry. Please. Please just let me go.'

'You're sorry?' the man said, walking around behind Jeff so he could no longer see him. 'Do you think that makes it all okay?'

'No. No, of course not.'

'Do you think any amount of apologising or repenting is going to make what you did — what you are — okay?'

Jeff gulped. 'No. No, I don't.'

The man was silent for a moment. 'Then there's only one thing for it, isn't there?'

He heard the rhythmic *snip, snip, snip* of the gardening shears before he saw the man walk back alongside him, lean down and begin to move the shears towards his naked penis.

'No! Please, no!' Jeff pleaded.

'Shh, we'll have no more of that,' the man said, pushing a stale rag into Jeff's mouth. 'We can't have you waking the neighbours, now, can we?'

The rhythmic sound of the shears started again.

*Snip, snip, snip.*

It was almost mesmerising, bewitching, and a deep part of Jeff's brain was actually quite enchanted by the sound up until the moment the steel blades crossed over his penis and the sound became a blistering sensation of searing pain.

Jeff could swear he felt at least one of his teeth crack as he bit down harder on the rag than he'd ever bitten on anything before.

'Oh, Jeff,' the man said. 'I think I understand your perversions now. You have no idea how much pleasure that just gave me. Sharp blades, aren't they?'

Jeff stared wide-eyed at the man as he opened up the jaws of the shears, now smeared with blood, and brought one open blade down towards his throat.

'Good fucking riddance, Jeff,' the man said, his teeth bared, before bringing the blade ripping across Jeff's throat with the movement and determination of a man trying to start a petrol lawnmower.

For Jeff Brelsford, the world suddenly got much darker.

## 3

Wendy Knight lay sprawled on the sofa, her head resting on her arm as the other stroked the purring cat which was similarly sprawled across her stomach.

The rehoming centre had told her the cat was called Cookie Monster, and said they tended to advise people to stick with the same name. Wendy was still unsure, though, and was sorely tempted to rename him. For now, though, she simply called him Cookie.

She felt daft saying it, but the cat had quickly become her closest friend and confidant. She'd gone to the rehoming centre shortly after the closure of the last murder case she'd worked on: the killing of four women in Milden-heath by a man who'd been trying to emulate the notorious crimes of Jack the Ripper.

The case had also resulted in the death of DS Luke Baxter, a young officer with the world at his feet. Wendy's relationship with Luke had been strained, to say the least, from the moment they'd met. Shortly before his death, though, they'd managed to clear the air and Wendy had finally felt that she understood him and had come to sympathise with and, dare she say it, quite like him.

Luke's death had dealt a hammer blow to Wendy and the entire CID department at Mildenheath. An officer dying in the line of duty was thankfully a rare occurrence in the UK at the best of times, and a largely desk-bound CID officer was even less likely to have to worry about being killed. For Luke Baxter, though, odds and probabilities meant nothing.

The funeral had been taken care of, with the local and national media attention on the event having been unprecedented. The force had tried to keep things as low-key as possible whilst giving Luke the send-off he deserved, but the attention that it had attracted from the media had made that difficult. A policeman dying in the line of duty was always bound to make headline news, but a CID officer being killed in the crossfire whilst apprehending one of the most brazen and daring serial killers of the modern age was something else altogether.

The death of a colleague wasn't something Wendy had experienced before, nor had most of the officers at Mildenheath, and she was surprised at the feelings it unlocked; feelings that took her back to the day she found out her own father had died.

Bill Knight had been a shining light at Mildenheath CID when Wendy was a young child, and had been off-duty when he'd tried to intervene and stop a bank robbery. She had never been told exactly what had happened next — she was too young at the time and hadn't wanted to ask since — but her father died of a gunshot wound later that day. 'Gone to join the angels,' her mother had said.

So many of the feelings and emotions she'd felt at the time had been kept under wraps — something she hadn't realised until now, when those feelings came flooding back. Oddly, she felt the same sense of the world having lost something. The conversation she'd had with Luke on the night of his death had changed the way she'd thought about him in a way which she was only realising now. She was sure that had Luke lived, they would've become good friends.

The whole of Mildenheath CID had been affected by Luke's death — some more than others — and Wendy had her concerns about one or two people who seemed to be taking it rather badly.

She moved her arm from behind her head and lifted the peaceful, purring Cookie from her lap and placed him on a cushion, stretching as she stood to go and fetch a bottle of wine from the wine rack. She'd perhaps been drinking a little too much lately, she'd be the first to admit, but she also knew she wasn't the only one. That was what the job did to you at the best of times, but at the worst of times it only became more of a necessity.

She looked back over her shoulder as she walked into the kitchen and could see Cookie stretching out and yawning before nodding back off into his peaceful slumber. She smiled as she thought what it would be like to be a cat, sleeping and eating without a care in the world. No worries about office politics, violent criminals or death. Just eat, sleep, rinse and repeat.

As the deep purple liquid sloshed into the wine glass, Wendy felt her mobile phone vibrating in her jeans pocket. She pulled it out and swiped across the screen to answer it, having seen the name of her superior, Detective Chief Inspector Jack Culverhouse, on the screen.

'Sir,' she said, keeping the greeting to a minimum as she knew Culverhouse would start speaking the second the line had connected.

'I hope you've not been on the sauce, Knight,' Culverhouse said immediately. 'We've got an incident to attend to.'

'What sort of incident?' she asked, knowing full-well that it would be nothing short of a dead body if a call had come through to her at this time of night.

'A fucking messy one,' he replied. 'Certainly not an accident, anyway. Not unless you can Taser yourself in the bollocks, chop your dick off and slit your throat by accident.'

'Jesus Christ. Got an address?'

'Yeah, Brunel Road.'

'Number?'

'Can't remember. It'll be the one with all the police cars outside. Want picking up on the way?'

Wendy laughed inwardly. Did she really sound drunk? 'Yeah, go on then. I've not even taken a mouthful yet, but seeing as you offered.'

## 4

He'd dreamt of the moment for years, but nothing could have prepared him for what it actually felt like to kill, to end a man's life. No, not a man. An animal. A monster.

That moment when he finally saw life being extinguished, the flicker die from behind Jeff Brelsford's eyes, had been a moment of purity and clarity for him. Suddenly, the world seemed a better place already.

He didn't feel bad, guilty or dirty about what he'd done; far from it. He knew he'd done a public service and, if he had to be completely honest with himself, he'd actually enjoyed it. He didn't think he would beforehand, and that had worried him. He had wondered whether he might feel a ceaseless sense of remorse and guilt afterwards, but he knew he'd have to cross that bridge when he came to it. Fortunately for him, he didn't look like he'd ever have to.

As far as he was concerned, the world was better off without Jeff Brelsford in it. Who knew how many young girls he would've gone on to groom, harass or abuse? The guilt he would've had to have lived with if he'd let Jeff Brelsford carry on breathing would have far outweighed any morsel of guilt he had over ending his life.

People like Jeff Brelsford could never change, he told himself. No-one ever heard of a paedophile coming out of prison, realising he was wrong and no longer being attracted to children. It just didn't happen. It was a disease; a disease of the mind, and one which had no cure. As far as he was concerned, that meant there was only one solution and that was the solution he'd brought the world in ending Jeff Brelsford's life.

Unfortunately, there were more men like Jeff Brelsford. Many more. The Dark Web forum he'd managed to infiltrate had taught him that. He'd thought Deepest Desires had been home to some pretty fucked up shit, but the new, un-named forum was on another level entirely.

What sickened him most was how the scumbags on the forum didn't even have the good grace to leer and slobber like he'd expected them to. Instead they used words such as 'gracious', 'petite' and 'elegant', as if they were talking about a particularly classy level of fashion model. It was like they didn't even know that it was a sick perversion, but some sort of sophisticated fetish or hobby instead.

The best thing about it is that no-one on the forum would know what had happened. For a start, he was the only one who knew that Celt_45 and Jeff Brelsford were one and the same person. Jeff Brelsford would be found — and probably mourned by at least one deluded idiot — but no-one would ever know Celt_45 was anything but alive and kicking. He knew this perfectly well as he would continue to post as Celt_45 himself, keeping the illusion alive until he could snare his second target.

The only thing that worried him was that he didn't know when he would stop. How do you know when the world is rid of perverts and paedophiles? Would it ever be? He'd always told himself that he'd carry on until he was caught.

The prospect of being caught didn't bother him in the slightest. It was one of the risks that came with the job. All jobs had their risks, and this was the one he took. What's the worst that could happen? He'd be sent to prison and be lauded as a hero. Sure, murderers weren't exactly up there with footballers and pop stars, but you'd be tough-pushed to find a bugger who wouldn't prefer them to a kiddy fiddler.

Nah, he'd be alright. You hear the stories about paedophiles being beaten up and abused in prison, so what would they make of him, the man who made it his mission to kill paedophiles? Prison certainly wouldn't be such a tough ride. Hell, it'd probably be easier than being on the outside. At least there he'd have respect. Extra dollop of mashed potato with his dinner. Lovely.

Whichever way you looked at it, he had only one option: Keep on keeping on.

## 5

The narrow road and tightly-packed Victorian houses gave Brunel Road a rather claustrophobic feel. It was the same as a number of roads in this area of Mildenheath, built before anyone could possibly have known how the motor car would impact on everyone's lives.

There were no driveways in sight and the tall, narrow houses had barely five-feet of front garden, meaning that around three houses were packed into the space that just one new home would occupy nowadays. As a result, getting parked anywhere nearby was something of a nightmare for Culverhouse.

The house itself had been sealed off at the front wall with police tape, a young constable standing guard just outside the boundaries of the property and another on the front door to the house. A number of neighbours were standing out in their front gardens, peering across to see what was going on.

Wendy walked ahead of Culverhouse, showed the officers her ID and entered the house, making her way through to the living room, where most of the action seemed to be taking place. Janet Grey, the pathologist, was already on the scene and was removing a pair of synthetic gloves as the pair entered.

'Seems there's someone keen to keep you in business,' the pathologist said. 'You've certainly got plenty to work on, anyway. Where do you want me to start?'

'Who found the body?' Wendy asked.

'Dog walker, believe it or not. She's being comforted back at home. Walked her dog past around nine forty-five and saw the front door half open with the hall light on. When she came back about half an hour later it was still open so she knocked and called inside.'

'There's your thanks for being a helpful neighbour, eh? Got any ID on our stiff?' Culverhouse asked, aiming his question at a uniformed officer stood over Janet Grey's shoulder.

'A Mr Jeff Brelsford, it seems. He's the sole occupier, anyway, according to the neighbours. Their descriptions of him seem to match as well.'

'Right. Which injury was the cause of death?'

'Probably the laceration to the throat,' the pathologist said. 'Fairly deep and nasty. Definitely forceful and deliberate. We're looking at someone who was pretty angry. Gone right through the trachea. I'd say from the blood splashes on his clothing he's probably coughed his own blood back up through the hole in his neck.'

'You know how to turn a man on, Dr Grey,' Culverhouse replied.

'The blood loss from the — well, the *amputation* — probably wouldn't have helped either.'

'I thought amputations were only limbs?' he asked.

'Doesn't make much difference to him. Would've bloody hurt either way. Of course, it's not for me to tell you how to do your job but I'd be wondering why the killer did that. You don't normally see gratuitous stuff like that without a reason. If you wanted him dead, you'd just kill him wouldn't you?'

'Depends what you wanted him dead for,' Wendy replied.

'Exactly. That'd be my first port of call.'

'So what, we're looking for a jilted ex-lover? Her father, perhaps?' Culverhouse asked.

'Perhaps. Oh, and someone with access to a Taser, too.'

'Was it definitely a Taser?' Culverhouse said.

'I'd say so personally, but we can't exactly narrow it down to a make and model like you can with gunshots. The lab monkeys might be able to identify it from the prong marks or determine a voltage from the burn pattern, but it's too early to say. Should at least be able to tell us whether or not it was police issue.'

'Police issue?' Culverhouse spluttered.

'Well, yeah. How many other people do you know who can just walk about with Tasers? Not exactly something you can just get from your local branch of Asda, is it?'

'No, but neither are guns and we've got no bloody shortage of them on the streets.'

'First steps, guv?' Wendy asked, keen to move the conversation on.

'Speak to the neighbours. We need to find out if anyone heard or saw anything. You can't just walk up to someone's front door and shoot them in the bollocks with a Taser without anyone noticing. Besides which, someone must've heard something. He'd've been kicking and screaming like no-one's business.'

'Ah, not necessarily,' Dr Grey interrupted. 'There's a pretty juicy knock to the back of the head, here. I'd say he hit his head going down after the Taser shot. Not something that could be planned, but still handy for the killer. Probably knocked him out for long enough for the killer to subdue him properly.'

'No signs of robbery at all? Nothing taken?' Culverhouse asked the uniformed officer.

'None, sir. Everything's pretty neat and tidy, actually. Wallet on the side in the kitchen with cash in it, TV and stuff still left here. Then again, if the killer came on foot, which I imagine he must've done around here, then there wouldn't be much chance for him to be taking stuff away with him.'

'Which means his primary intention presumably wasn't to rob the place,' Culverhouse said.

'They were my first thoughts, sir, I must admit,' the officer said.

Culverhouse looked at him benevolently for a few moments; a look Wendy hadn't seen from him in a long, long time.

'You'll go a long way, son,' he said, before turning to look back at the corpse of Jeff Brelsford. 'Right, Knight. Looks like I've got an incident room to set up. I'll leave you to speak with the neighbours.'

As Wendy left Jeff Brelsford's house and stood outside to survey the scene, a man from the house opposite crossed the road to speak to her.

'You are a detective?' he asked. Wendy sensed a strong Eastern European lilt to his voice. 'My name is Marius, I live across road. I think I saw who killed him.'

## 6

Marius's house was remarkably similar to Jeff Brelsford's. She presumed most of the houses in the street and on the estate would be fairly identical, save for a few extensions or knocked-through interior walls.

Once Wendy had politely declined a cup of tea and managed to steer the conversation away from how much Marius had wanted to be a policeman in Romania but could never pass the exams, he began to tell her what he'd seen.

'I went out to my bin, and I saw a man dressed in a black suit. He was just turning into Jeff's garden, through gate and walked to door.'

'Did you see his face?'

'No, no face. Only back of his head.'

'What did it look like? What colour hair?'

Marius grimaced slightly. 'I am not sure. Dark hair, I

think, and not long hair, but is dark outside and there is no... How you say?' he replied, waving his hand in the air.

'Streetlight?'

'Yes, streetlight. Is not one outside his house, and I was not wearing my glasses.'

Wendy smiled, although inside she was a little frustrated. 'Did you see him go inside the house?'

'No, I went back inside. I did not think was weird, just maybe a visitor or friend. Nothing special.'

'What time was this?' Wendy asked.

Marius narrowed his eyebrows. 'About eight o'clock, I think.'

'And did you see this man leave?'

Marius shook his head. 'No, I did not think was strange, so I went inside. I did not hear anything.' He seemed to be genuinely worried that Wendy would be angry, as if she'd arrest him for not being a more observant neighbour. It occurred to her that perhaps policing was done somewhat differently in Romania.

'Don't worry, it's absolutely fine and understandable. Believe me, you've been a lot more helpful than most neighbours. You'd be amazed what people don't see going on right outside their own homes. People just keep themselves to themselves. They don't look out for each other any more.'

Marius just smiled, as if he didn't quite know what to say.

. . .

As Wendy left Marius's house, the uniformed officer stood outside the police cordon told her that Jeff Brelsford's neighbours, Chloe Downie and Harry Kendrick, had just got home, having been out for the evening.

Wendy made her way over to their house and knocked on the door. A young man, surely no older than his late teens or early twenties at most, opened the door and pushed his fringe away from his eyes.

'Harry Kendrick? My name's Detective Sergeant Wendy Knight, from Mildenheath CID. My colleague said he spoke to you briefly.'

'Yeah, yeah. Come in,' Harry said, stepping aside to let Wendy through.

'This is my girlfriend, Chloe,' he said, gesturing to her as they entered the living room. Chloe smiled.

'So, did you know Jeff Brelsford at all?' Wendy asked.

'Nah, not really,' Harry replied. 'I mean we saw him every now and again, what with living next door to him, but we've only rented the place four months so far and we're mostly out working.'

'Don't often get to go out together, even in the evenings,' Chloe said. 'We went to see a film.'

Wendy smiled ruefully. It was such a shame that a young couple, clearly devoted enough to each other to want to set up home, were spending so much time working to keep that home that they barely got to spend any time with each other.

'Did many people come and go from his house? Friends, girlfriends, anything like that?'

Harry and Chloe looked at each other momentarily. 'No, I don't think so,' Harry said. 'To be honest, we never really heard much from him. No music or anything like that, even. That surprised me, actually, as you would've thought we'd hear something through these walls. We can even hear the old woman the other side of us coughing,' he added, lowering his voice almost to a whisper just in case the woman next door could hear him, too.

'Very thin walls,' Chloe said. 'To be honest, it's a bit creepy, actually, knowing that people next door can hear everything. We have to be a bit... Well, careful, if you see what I mean. At night.'

'Yes, I understand,' Wendy said, trying to change the conversation. 'And was there anything odd over the last few days and weeks at all? New cars on the street, people hanging round, Jeff acting differently perhaps?'

Harry shook his head. 'Not that we've noticed. But then we've both hardly been around. We've been so preoccupied with work, I doubt we would've noticed if all of those things had happened. Sorry, we're probably not being much help.'

. . .

Having left Harry and Chloe with her phone number should they remember anything and want to contact her, Wendy decided to try the neighbour on the other side of Jeff Brelsford's house.

The elderly man who opened the door looked visibly upset at the news he'd received barely an hour earlier. He guided Wendy into his living room, where she found a woman sobbing into a handkerchief.

'I'm afraid my wife is rather upset about it all. You see, she's hard of hearing so we had the television on very loud, as we always do. Poor girl reckons it was her fault now and that if we'd had the telly down lower we might have heard the chap shouting or something. No use me trying to tell her that with her ears she wouldn't have heard the telly or the bloke. She won't have it.'

'It's the shock, I'm sure,' Wendy said, sitting down on the sofa next to the man's wife and putting a reassuring hand on her shoulder. 'What did you say your names were?' she said to the man.

'I didn't. I'm Des Forrester. My wife is Joy.'

Not much Joy about her at the moment, Wendy thought. 'Did you know Jeff Brelsford personally?' she asked.

Joy carried on crying as Des spoke. 'No, not really. We went round and introduced ourselves when he moved in, but we're old-fashioned like that. Other than a quick hello over the garden wall if we happened to be out at the same time, that was about it. Sad, isn't it, how society's changed?'

Wendy simply smiled. 'Had anything different happened recently? Anything a little out of the ordinary, new people around, that sort of thing?'

'Not that I can think of,' Des replied. 'What about you, love?' he shouted towards his wife. 'Did you notice anything odd happening around here recently?'

Joy shook her head between sobs.

'Nothing at all?' he yelled. 'Anything?'

By now, Wendy's ears were ringing and she wondered if perhaps she'd be the next one to go deaf if she had to take any more of this.

'Perhaps I could leave my card and you could give me a call if either of you think of anything.'

'Yes, good idea,' Des said, looking at the card and seeming to read every word. 'We'll have a think and let you know.'

Wendy had to agree with Des Forrester. It was quite sad that no-one really spoke to or acknowledged their neighbours any more. It wasn't just a case of lives getting busier and it being a shame, but the fact that this modern ignorance and style of insular living could quite possibly have cost a man his life.

Culverhouse had let her know that there'd be an incident room meeting in the morning and that there wasn't much else they could do at that time of night. The forensics team would be working through the night to gather evidence, which would give them something to discuss in the morning.

Feeling reinvigorated yet apprehensive, and wanting to get back before midnight, Wendy decided to head for home. That bottle of wine was starting to look even more appealing.

## 7

Wendy had thought that perhaps a new morning would bring fresh hope, but a distinct lack of sleep had put paid to that.

She'd lain awake for most of the night thinking about the scene she'd witnessed at Jeff Brelsford's house. No matter how many crime scenes she saw, she never quite managed to get over the sense of sorrow she felt. Every dead body was a brother, sister, mother, father, son or daughter. It was a friend, a neighbour, a colleague. Every one had a story to tell, but their final story was her job to uncover.

Her walk from the car park into the staff entrance of Mildenheath Police Station was one which had been tinged with sadness ever since Luke Baxter's death. At the entrance was a brass plaque, which read *In memory of DS Luke Baxter* above his dates of birth and death. It was something which saddened her every time she saw it, yet she knew it was completely right that every officer should remember Luke, what he sacrificed and the potential dangers to their own lives every time they showed up for work.

Wendy felt she was coping. It was something that had become second nature in her life since her parents died and her brother became a drug addict and subsequently murdered her partner and tried to kill her. Her miscarriage not long after had been a huge hammer blow. Plus, of course, there was the career history of dealing with violent murders and crimes which left its unavoidable mark on her. Wendy had learnt to cope. There was no other way. She was a professional coper.

For Jack Culverhouse, though, things were different. Wendy had noticed some marked changes in his behaviour recently. The brash, macho exterior and jokey ways had continued, but she knew him well enough to know that it was all bravado, a cover which hid the true feelings beneath. True enough, she suspected that had always been the case but she also knew that he was hurting far more deeply than he let on. After all, Luke had quite literally sacrificed his life for him by throwing himself in front of the bullet that was meant for his superior officer.

He'd been drinking heavily and there were whisperings that words had been had at higher levels. The problem was that Jack Culverhouse was more than functioning as a

CID officer. He was the best around, there was no doubt about it, and as a result he got away with far, far more than anyone else in the same position would ever do.

The incident room was worryingly familiar to Wendy. Culverhouse would be running the shop as always, with her effectively being his second in command. Alongside them were DS Frank Vine, DS Steve Wing and DC Debbie Weston.

Luke's death had left a hole in the team, and the negative ramifications ran much deeper for Mildenheath CID. For a while now, the county police headquarters at Milton House had been home to the regionalised CID department. Mildenheath was the only town that had managed to hold on to its own CID team, partially because of the high serious crime rate in the town but also largely due to the sheer stubbornness of Jack Culverhouse and the Chief Constable, Charles Hawes, who had come up through the ranks at Mildenheath. Hawes was quite happy to have an office at the station, well out of the way of the county's Police and Crime Commissioner, Martin Cummings, with whom he didn't enjoy a good relationship to say the least.

The fact of the matter was that Mildenheath CID was now one man smaller than it had been, and before long it would be impossible to argue against it being subsumed into Milton House — something that DCI Malcolm Pope, Culverhouse's opposite number and nemesis, was waiting for with bated breath. Although Luke's death wasn't a situation anyone could have planned, no-one at Mildenheath CID would put it past Martin Cummings to use it to his political advantage. Regardless, Jack Culverhouse was ploughing on and was getting stuck into the morning briefing.

As he made his way to the front of the room to address the team, a ball of scrunched-up paper bounced off the corner of a desk and hit his leg.

'Who the fuck was that?' he barked.

'Sorry, guv,' came the voice of DS Steve Wing. 'I was aiming for the bin. I should've got up and put it in properly. Sorry.'

'No, you should've aimed better and not thrown like a girl,' Culverhouse replied, picking up the paper and walking over to where Steve was sitting. 'Get up.'

Steve did as he was told. Culverhouse sat down in Steve's chair, which was a good twenty feet away from the waste paper basket, lifted his hand and propelled the scrunched-up ball of paper through a perfect trajectory and into the bin without even hitting the edge.

'Like that,' he said, standing up and returning to his spot at the front of the room.

'Bloody hell, guv. You should get on the force's cricket team. They could do with a couple of decent bowlers.'

'No chance,' Culverhouse replied. 'I'd be too tempted to launch every ball at Malcolm Pope's head. Right. Murder case. We now know that the victim is Jeff Brelsford, a forty-eight-year-old local man who lived alone in a rented house. Turns out he's known to us. He's listed on ViSOR.'

The Violent and Sex Offenders Register listed the details of all people convicted of a crime or receiving a caution under the 2003 Sexual Offences Act in England and Wales and those thought to be at risk of offending.

'That would probably go some way towards explaining the way he was killed,' Culverhouse added.

'What was he on the register for, guv?' Debbie Weston asked.

'He was cautioned for sexual harassment at work last year. He used to work for a company doing car body repairs and a school-leaver reported him for sexual harassment a fortnight into her working there.'

'Christ. How old was she?' Debbie asked.

'Sixteen. Now, Tasering someone in the bollocks and chopping their cock off seems to have a pretty clear message, wouldn't you say?'

'What, you think it was someone connected with the girl he molested?' Steve Wing asked.

'I'd say it's more than possible. Either that or he's been up to his old tricks again and someone took a dislike to it.'

'Could even be some sort of vigilante thing,' Debbie added. 'Especially if he's on ViSOR.'

'Only problem with that is that it's only the police, NPS and HMPS who have access to ViSOR, which would narrow the field a bit. From what we can tell there's no immediate family in the area. Never married, no kids. Probably for the best, if you ask me.'

'I'll get in touch with the family of the girl he assaulted,' Wendy said. 'Probably best that we get a statement from them and find out where they were last night.'

Culverhouse snorted and crossed his arms. 'If you find out one of them did it, shake their hand for me.'

8

It was all about trust. Once you'd gained that, you could pretty much do what you liked with them. The rest was pure psychology.

Building trust was difficult. The increasingly volatile attitudes towards people like the ones he was targeting meant that they were naturally suspicious of everyone. The police's increasing resources and computer forensics teams made their lives more difficult and increased suspicions enormously.

This meant that a number of them had fragmented and were left to satisfy their perversions alone, safe from the potential of misplaced trust. These were the low-hanging fruit, the marginals who were easy to pick off but far less fun. Some parts of the community, on the other hand, had come together more closely, forming small groups of people who could trust each other implicitly. That sort of faith took a long time to build up, but it was worth all the effort. These were the group he'd effectively formed, ensuring a tight circle around their rotten cores.

He had to play the long game. Finding a paedophile wasn't particularly difficult in the modern age of the internet, but any criminal of any sort who drew that much attention to himself wasn't one worth bothering with. As with anything, it was the quiet ones you had to watch out for. It was the ones who had driven themselves underground, going to great lengths to mask their activities. It's the same principle that says the door with the biggest lock has the most treasure behind it.

Getting on side was difficult, but the primary tactic was to display suspicion himself. He knew that you couldn't simply make another person trust you, but you could make them want you to trust them. That would have much the same effect with the added advantage that effectively they'd be the ones grovelling and coming to him. That put him in an additional position of power.

It had taken months, years in some cases, but every second was worth it. He'd had to use a variety of tactics. Simple faith-building hadn't always worked, and every person had a limit to the amount of certitude they could have in another human being. Sure enough, some had been daft enough to eventually reveal their locations or real names in one way or another, but for some that task was far more difficult and had to be done in different ways.

There were some who were really hot on their security. Those who only used VPNs, connected through the TOR network and used anonymous email accounts on the Dark Web with PGP encryption. They were the very core of the nut he wanted to crack, but getting past that level of security would be next to impossible.

The next level down was where the fun was really had: those who weren't going to voluntarily give up any information, but who were slightly less security conscious and made the occasional technological slip-up. Those, for example, who used a Gmail or Hotmail email account, thinking it anonymous and throwaway. To an extent, it was, but he had his ways and means.

One of the most successful tactics was to send links to the sort of depraved material they got their kicks out of — something he hated doing, but which was entirely necessary in pursuit of the greater good — which would build up their trust. The occasional link would be to a web server he owned or of which he had access to the logs. As soon as the link was clicked, he'd be able to see the person's IP address. More often than not, they'd be behind a VPN or using TOR, but everyone would slip up sooner or later. When they did, their cover had essentially been blown.

Having their IP address would, in some cases, give him a fairly specific geographic location which would narrow the field enormously. In other cases, he could use that to his advantage in other ways. If the IP address only told him the person was in Nottingham, for example, he'd send them an email purporting to be from Nottingham City Council announcing big council tax rises or changes to their bin collection dates. The email would contain a link to a website mocked up to look like Nottingham City Council's website, asking the user to enter their postcode and house number to find out their new council tax payment or bin collection date. Bingo. He had their address.

With their address, it was only one step to finding out their name. Often, a Google search would tell him. If they'd signed an online petition, their name would often accompany their address in a search result. If a business was registered to the address, he could find out the directors' names. If they owned the property, he could look up the title deeds. If all else failed, rocking up at the house pretending to be from the gas board or water company would often do the trick.

Once he had a name and address, he was home and dry. More information was always handy, but he could go a long way with this. If he found out the person's place of work, date of birth or more, he could get to know their lives, their daily routines. If not, simple personal surveillance would often do the trick.

The fact was that most of them were spread out across

the country. As the group grew, though, the number of targets living within a reasonable distance grew too. By now, he had a solid core of targets who didn't live far away at all, and who would all be feeling the full force of his own special brand of justice very soon indeed.

## 9

Jack Culverhouse always had mixed feelings when he was asked to go to the Chief Constable's office. It would almost always be bad news, but Culverhouse was eternally grateful that it was Charles Hawes who was Chief Constable and not anyone else.

Hawes knew what it was like to police on the front line and had been through Mildenheath CID himself, working in Jack's position before him. Hawes let him get away with a lot more than anyone else would, and that wasn't lost on him. The pair were united by a distrust — verging on hatred — of the elected Police and Crime Commissioner, Martin Cummings, who'd brought politics into policing far more than it had any right to be. They were also both inherently suspicious of Malcolm Pope, the man who headed up the CID department at the county's policing headquarters at Milton House.

Milton House was a good twenty or so miles away from Mildenheath, which was just far enough for Charles Hawes to justify having an office at both locations, preferring to spend as much time at Mildenheath as possible. The real reason was that it put him twenty miles further away from Martin Cummings and the needless bureaucracy at county hall, but the official reasoning was that Mildenheath had good media facilities, was more accessible to local press and was right on the doorstep of the majority of the county's crime. Handily, Hawes could sell this as getting his hands dirty and putting himself right in the thick of it, although that was actually far from the truth.

Culverhouse saw Hawes as a good blend of old school policing and modern advancements. He was firm but fair: something Culverhouse always aspired to, although he never quite managed to strike the right balance. To Charles Hawes, what mattered was the result and keeping a clean image. He was willing to allow a few rules to be bent if it meant them getting their man and stopping more people from being harmed. After all, that was everyone's ultimate goal.

Although Culverhouse knew he wasn't being summoned for a pay rise or a pat on the back, Hawes's office felt like a sanctuary to him as he closed the door behind him and sat down on the other side of the ornate mahogany desk from the Chief Constable.

'You and I go back a long way, Jack,' Hawes said, reassuring Culverhouse that this was certainly not going to result in a pay rise. 'I know what things are like in your position. I've been there. I've seen it all. And I know that sometimes personal feelings and reflections can take over, especially since... Well, you know.'

Culverhouse flared his nostrils. Could the man not even bring himself to say Luke's name?

'I'm not sure I know what you mean, sir,' Culverhouse said, more politely than he felt like saying it.

'Well, recent events. Things have been tough on everyone here. I understand that. But it's vital that everyone keeps a level head. Even things said in the incident room can sway the way people think. The last thing we need is for personal feelings and disagreements to get in the way of operations.'

Culverhouse shook his head. 'Sorry. I must be missing something. What are you talking about?'

The Chief Constable sighed. 'It was reported to me that you may or may not have made a remark about the death of Jeff Brelsford. Something to do with congratulating his killer. Ring any bells?'

Culverhouse loosened his jaw, trying to stop his teeth from clenching so tightly. 'May I ask who?'

'No, Jack, because it's important that officers can express their feelings in confidence.'

'Right. But I'm not allowed to express mine?'

'Yes, of course you are. Privately. To me. Like we are right now, and like that other officer did. Not in a team briefing and not in the way you did. If you did, that is.'

'And what if I did?' he asked. 'What does that have to do with catching whoever killed him?'

Charles Hawes sighed again. 'Listen, Jack. I'm going to put this bluntly. You know I'm good for overlooking one or two smaller issues which others might pick up on. I like to see a CID department flowing as a unit under its own steam rather than trampling all over it. But the fact of the matter is I'm not going to be here forever. I'm getting older, Jack, and I'm going to have to think about retirement pretty soon before they think of it for me. I don't know who they'll get in to replace me, but one thing I know for sure is there's no way whoever it is will have the same outlook as me. We're the last of the old school, you and me. I hate to break it to you, but you wouldn't last five minutes under another Chief Constable. You'd be fired for gross misconduct within a week.'

He knew the Chief Constable was right, but ignored the point. 'Sir, if you've got concerns then I don't think I should be the senior investigating officer on this case. A lot has happened recently. I wouldn't want my personal feelings to get in the way of operations,' he added through gritted teeth.

Hawes steepled his hands and rested his mouth against

his fingers. 'I see. Well, that's a very brave move to make, I must say.'

'I'm happy to work on the case if you want me to, or not. Whatever. We've got plenty of people who can run the team. Put Knight on it.'

'She's only a DS, Jack. We can't have her as SIO.'

'Promote her then.'

'It doesn't work like that, Jack. You know it doesn't. It's no good being flippant. If you step down as senior investigating officer, another DCI will have to take charge. And you and I both know who that'd be.'

Culverhouse nodded. Neither of the men wanted to sully the air with Malcolm Pope's name.

'The question is, Jack, are you strong enough, up here,' he said, tapping his temple with a forefinger, 'to handle things as they are right now?'

Culverhouse moved his tongue around his teeth before answering. 'I don't do giving up.'

## 10

Katie McCourt's parents hadn't been hugely keen on the idea of speaking to the police about Jeff Brelsford again, but she had agreed to meet with Wendy to help in any way she could with the investigation into his death.

From what Wendy had read about on the police national computer, Jeff Brelsford's caution came after two prior warnings about his behaviour. Katie McCourt was apparently not the sort of girl to take prisoners and had reported Brelsford after the first instance of harassment. It seemed the warnings hadn't quite got through to him, though, and he had to be spoken to twice more before he finally got the message.

The first and second times, he had been making advances and lewd comments. The third time, though, he'd attempted to grope her and kiss her. Considering that he was a man who was more than twice her age at the time,

Katie had been extremely distressed and had insisted that the police do something.

With a lack of witnesses on hand, the Crown Prosecution Service weren't particularly interested, but Brelsford had agreed to accept a police caution for his behaviour, having seemed genuinely remorseful. Katie had been happy, too, knowing that Brelsford would lose his job and have to sign on to the sex offender's register. According to the notes, she considered that fair justice.

Although Wendy had requested the company of Debbie Weston as the trained family liaison officer in order to ensure that everything was dealt with as sensitively as possible, Culverhouse had decided that Debbie's efforts would be better spent elsewhere and that Wendy should speak to Katie and her family members on her own. With the atmosphere in the incident room the way it was at that moment, she was secretly quite glad to be able to get out for a bit.

Wendy was also quite pleased that Katie was at work when she went to visit her parents, as she liked to try and speak to people separately where she could. People tended to be more open and honest one-to-one, whereas they often seemed to clam up a bit in front of others, particularly parents and particularly when talking about a sensitive subject such as sexual assault.

Katie McCourt's parents lived in a smart detached property on Yardley Crescent, not a million miles from

Wendy's relatively humble abode in Archer's Close. John and Teresa welcomed Wendy in, offered her a cup of tea and sat down at the kitchen table. It was a well-looked-after house and they were clearly proud people. Up until last year, she supposed, they probably wouldn't have had very many dealings with the police at all. After what had happened to their daughter, though, welcoming a CID detective into the kitchen didn't seem quite so odd.

On the phone earlier, Wendy had decided not to hedge around the point and got straight to telling John and Teresa that the man who'd sexually harassed their daughter had been found murdered in his home the previous evening. Teresa seemed shocked; John emotionless.

'There's no easy way of me saying this,' Wendy said, 'but whenever someone is murdered the first thing we have to do is look at anyone who might've wanted them dead. I know that might—'

'No, no, we quite understand,' John said, looking at his wife for reassurance. 'I can see why you're here.'

Wendy smiled, pleased that they seemed so understanding. It could have been a lot more awkward to turn up on the doorstep of the parents of a sexual harassment victim and tell them they were the prime suspects in the murder of their daughter's harasser.

'I suppose you're going to want alibis,' Katie's father said. 'We were both at home all night. Katie finished work around six-thirty — she's on a daytime shift at the moment — and she was back here about twenty minutes later.'

'Did she stay in all night?' Wendy asked.

John McCourt told her she did.

'And where does she work at the moment?'

'At the hospital. She's been working as a receptionist in A&E for the past couple of months or so. It's shift work, mostly. Some days she finishes at six-thirty, others she's not back until late. If she does a night shift it's even later.'

'Must be tough work,' Wendy said, attempting to build some empathy.

'It is, but she finds it rewarding.'

'And how's she coping now, after what happened with Jeff Brelsford?'

'The fact that he's dead, you mean? We've not seen her since we found out. If you mean how's she been since he got the police caution, she's a very resilient person. She doesn't let things like that affect her too much. Not on the surface, anyway.'

'She's less trusting,' Teresa said, speaking for the first time since Wendy had arrived.

'I suppose she is, yes,' John said, looking at Teresa. 'It clearly knocked her a bit. She left the job as soon as she could. Certainly wasn't a nice atmosphere at that place. She took some time to work out what she wanted to do, did some shifts at the pub round the corner, the Spitfire, then decided she fancied the look of this job at the hospital.'

'She's talked about training as a nurse,' Teresa said. 'She wants to help people.'

'And what are your feelings towards Jeff Brelsford?' Wendy said, trying to steer the conversation back towards something useful.

'If you're asking whether we're glad he's dead, then I've got to tell you I don't know. I hated the bloke for what he did to my daughter, but I'm not the sort of person who wishes death on people.'

'And you, Mrs McCourt?' Wendy said to Katie's mother.

Teresa looked at John. 'I agree with John. I don't know what to think, to be honest. I must admit that my first reaction was "Oh good", though. I wasn't his biggest fan, put it that way.'

John took Teresa's hand in his and squeezed it.

Wendy could see that the impact an event like that had on a family was far deeper and further reaching than what was on the surface level. Knowing that your daughter had been violated in that way must cut deep, and even the most forgiving people would find it difficult not to rejoice in the knowledge that the person who did it wouldn't be able to offend again.

'I mean, it could have been much worse,' John said. 'He obviously wasn't the sort of person to stop, even after a couple of warnings. You never know how far he would've gone if he'd managed to get her on her own or something.

What if he'd put something in her drink at a Christmas party or something? I know it sounds mad, but you never know how far people like that will go.'

Wendy started to detect that perhaps John McCourt held a little more animosity towards Jeff Brelsford than he had admitted.

## 11

Jack could feel the blood pulsing in his temples as he made his way down the stairs from the Chief Constable's office. His rough, jagged fingernails cut into the palms of his hands as he clenched his fists, his thoughts making a whirring, buzzing noise as they bounced around inside his skull.

He jammed his hand down on the handle of the incident room's door and flung it open, listening to it crash against the wall, the handle embedding in the plasterboard, wedging it in place.

The room fell silent.

'Go on, then,' he said quietly, almost whispered. 'Who was it?'

Some pairs of eyes looked at him with concern, others were averted towards the floor.

'Who was it?' he yelled, the volume making at least two other officers jump before his voice returned back to its whisper. 'The only reason you lot are here, the sole reason you're working in the only CID department in this half of the country that hasn't become a faceless office block at county hall, is because I have had the bollocks to stand up and be counted. Because I have single-fucking-handedly put more serious criminals behind bars than the lot of you put together. Because I get results. And now — now — I hear that one of you has gone behind my back and told the Chief Constable that you have *concerns* about my methods and opinions.'

He took a moment to survey the incident room. All eyes were now averted away from him.

'You have your jobs because people like me are willing to do things a bit differently. Because we put justice and safety before pen-pushing and fucking bureaucracy. While you're busy filling in forms, reaching targets and having appraisals, at least one of you would do very well to remember that it was my way of doing things which means you're stood here living and breathing today.' He didn't look at Debbie Weston as he spoke, but he could tell she knew who he was talking about. 'And because of another officer's bravery and selflessness, and his willingness to throw himself quite literally into the firing line, you're still breathing lungfuls of God's own.'

Culverhouse spoke now through a growing fog of tears. 'Have a think for just one second where you'd be if officers like Luke had been sat here filling in fucking paperwork instead of doing what he had to do that day. And then tell me that you're right to criticise the way I do things. Because the way I do things fucking *works*,' he yelled, smashing his fist down on the nearest desk. 'Whether you like it or not, it's the reason you're here and the sole reason why at least one of you is still alive. Now. I'm going to ask again. Who was it?'

Before anyone could answer, the voice of the Chief Constable spoke from the open doorway. 'Jack. A word.'

Without even acknowledging Charles Hawes, Culverhouse looked at each one of the officers in the incident room before turning and following him out.

They'd barely got three steps out of the office when Hawes rounded on him.

'I'm going to cut to the chase, Jack, and you're going to listen. Collect your stuff and go home. I'm putting you on indefinite leave. No ifs, no buts. You're not in the right frame of mind right now and I can't risk having you around here.'

Hawes looked at Culverhouse, expecting him to come back aggressively, but instead he just stood there devoid of any expression. 'Right now, Jack, you're toxic. You're going to do more harm than good to this investigation, by a long way. You're a good officer. I know that and you know that, but you need time. It's understandable. We all do sometimes. Do you understand?'

Culverhouse said nothing, turned around and headed for the exit.

## 12

The hospital canteen was almost as bad as the one at the station, so Wendy felt very much at home. Katie McCourt, though, looked less than pleased at having had the past dragged up again. She twisted a piece of tissue around her finger as she stared at the steaming styrofoam mug of tea.

'I realise it's difficult to have to go through things again,' Wendy said. 'Especially after having consigned them to the past. But I hope you'll understand that we need to look at things with a fresh pair of eyes in light of... Well, recent developments.'

Katie kept staring at the tea and was silent for a few moments before she started talking.

'I know it sounds ridiculous to say it, but I feel nothing towards him. I don't hate him. I never wished him dead. I think more than anything I feel sorry for him.'

Wendy smiled with one side of her mouth. 'You'd be

surprised how many people say that.'

'I think it's the feeling of violation that hurts the most. It's like when people have their houses burgled, they say it's not the material stuff that matters. They don't really care that someone's nicked their telly or their laptop or whatever. It's knowing that someone's been in their house uninvited when they weren't there, rummaging through their stuff.'

'I know exactly what you mean,' Wendy said. 'And I'm really sorry to have to ask you this, but it's something I have to do as part of the job...'

'Before you ask, I was home around seven-ish and stayed in all night,' Katie said, making eye contact with Wendy for the first time since Wendy had told her what had happened. She could see not only the determination in Katie's eyes, but also that what she was telling her was the truth.

'What about other people?' Wendy asked. 'Friends, family? Did any of them express a wish to see Jeff Brelsford dead?'

Katie laughed and shook her head before wiping her eyes. 'Is that a serious question? For a start it wasn't exactly something I went and broadcast everywhere. I only told my family and close friends. Anyone who was that close to me was obviously going to hate him for what he did. But no, none of them would've actually done anything to him.'

Wendy pursed her lips. 'I hate to ask this, but can you

be sure?'

'Yes, I can. It's not as if it happened just recently and someone snapped and acted in anger, is it? There's been plenty of time for people to deal with it and if I can move on I'm sure my friends and family can. In fact, I know they can. They have.'

One thing that Wendy always tried to do was to put herself in the victim's shoes. It tended to help her to empathise with what they'd been through and to know the best way to approach a situation. Then she could combine that with her duties as a police officer. It was an approach which had been very successful, she thought.

Trying to get into Katie McCourt's mind was some-what more difficult, though. Katie's experiences with Jeff Brelsford hadn't been as serious as many others she encountered in her job as a police officer — far from it — but for Katie it had clearly had a big impact on her life.

Wendy never failed to be surprised by the ways in which people reacted to different situations. There were some for whom a serious assault or violent robbery could be — relatively speaking — brushed under the carpet and put down to experience, but then there were others for whom having their mobile phone nicked from a table in a pub or finding their car broken into could have a devas-tating impact. It was all personal and subjective, and any crime could feel deeply personal to any given person. And, right now, that was what worried Wendy the most.

## 13

Jack poured another measure of scotch into his glass, carefully put the bottle back on the table and took a gulp. He'd usually expect to feel the clatter of ice cubes against his teeth as he savoured the flavour, but this time the whisky served a very different purpose altogether.

This was all about dulling the pain. Not only the pain and shame of being put on leave from work, but of everything that had led up to that. Every man had a breaking point, he knew that, but it was also true that the deeper your breaking point was, the more damage it'd cause when it finally went.

The stress of work was barely the surface level. Below that was the way in which Luke's death had affected him — something he'd never even considered acknowledging, particularly not at work. He'd always admired Luke's dedication to the job and saw a large amount of his younger self in Luke. He'd believed in him, encouraged him, mentored him and then watched him take a bullet for him. A bullet that had ended his life. In many ways, Jack felt as if his life had ended then too. Had Luke not been there, only his own life would have been lost — something he felt was now lost anyway — and Luke's would've been spared.

He wondered, too, if he had made the right decision in going to that house with Luke in the first place, having done so to rescue Debbie Weston, who was being held hostage. Logically he knew they'd done the right thing in coming to Debbie's rescue, but that decision had condemned Luke to his fate. Of course, there was no way he could've known that at the time. Hindsight is a wonderful thing, he thought.

He worried at how much his decision making at that time had been hindered by what he was going through in his personal life, his mentally unstable ex-wife having appeared back on the scene eight and a half years after disappearing one day with their daughter, who he'd still not seen since. That kind of pressure took its toll, no matter how strong a person you were.

The ringing of the doorbell jolted him from his intro-spection but he had no intention of answering it. After three rings, he heard the letterbox open.

'Guv, it's me,' called the familiar voice of Wendy Knight. 'I know you're in there. And I know you're hurting. We all are. Let me in and we can talk about it. As friends.'

That word resonated. Jack had never had friends. Not really. He'd always told himself he wasn't the friend type. He didn't need them. Right now, though, he was starting to wonder if that was true.

'Look, the others told me what happened. I don't like seeing you like this. I'm worried.'

Jack swallowed as a tear rolled down his cheek. He slowly stood up and made his way to the front door, unlatching it but not opening it, before sitting back down where he'd been.

Wendy opened the door, closed it behind her and went into the living room.

'How are you?' she asked, not knowing what else to say.

'How do I look?'

'Shit.'

'Got it in one.'

Wendy allowed herself a wry smile. 'That's not going to help,' she said, pointing at the bottle of scotch.

'It's certainly not doing me any harm right now,' he replied, taking another gulp.

'Not that you know of. It's not going to let you think clearly, though, is it?'

Jack sighed. 'I don't want to think clearly. I don't want to think at all.'

Wendy sat down on the sofa next to him. 'I get that. I

do. It's natural. But you need people who can help you get through it.'

Jack shook his head. 'I'm too old for all this. There's only so much one man can take. Even me. Even Jack fucking Culverhouse.'

'What do you mean?' Wendy asked, cocking her head.

'I mean I'm going to offer my resignation to the Chief Constable. Officially. I'm retiring.'

Wendy's eyes widened. 'What? No, you can't. You—'

'I can, and I am. That way I'll still keep my pension intact. If I carry on and cross the wrong line, I'll lose everything. It's all I've got left as it is.'

Wendy closed her eyes and sighed. She knew his decision would be eminently sensible for most people, but it wasn't a way forward for Jack. He wasn't a man who did cutting his losses. He was a fighter, someone who rallied against perceived injustices and came out on top even stronger than before.

'I think you should speak to someone,' she said. 'A professional. Someone who can help you make sense of everything. I know it might seem like you're thinking clearly and rationally right now, but you can't be. You've been through a lot. If you speak to a professional, you can get through this.'

'I am not seeing a fucking shrink,' he replied, with a little too much venom in his voice for Wendy's liking.

'It'd help. Trust me. I've been there,' she said,

neglecting to mention the fact that the only two times she'd been in a counsellor's office she'd stormed out in a fit of denial in much the same way Jack was doing now.

'It's not going to happen, Knight. I'm finished. I'm done. And you should leave.'

'Seriously? Do you think that's going to help?' Wendy asked, now at her wits' end.

Jack sighed. 'I don't know, and right now I don't care.'

'What about Luke's memorial service?' Wendy asked quietly.

He bowed his head and turned away. 'I don't know. I really don't know. I don't know if I can handle it right now.'

'With all due respect, you don't get a say as to when it is. You need to be there. The whole reason it's happening is because he saved your life. We need to honour that. Honour him.'

He turned back to face Wendy, all emotion drained from his face. 'No. There's nothing to honour. It should've been me who died that day.'

## 14

The arrival of Malcolm Pope at Mildenheath Police Station was always guaranteed to turn the atmosphere somewhat frostier, even though it was thankfully a relatively rare occurrence. This time, everyone in CID knew that his stay was going to be prolonged.

Within twenty minutes of his arrival, he was stood at the front of the incident room, addressing the team.

'Now, I've been briefed on what's happened so far and, unsurprisingly, it doesn't seem to be much. I understand everything you've all been through and the pressures you've been under, but the facts aren't altered: we have a murder victim who deserves the truth.'

Wendy nodded ever so slightly. She was far from Malcolm Pope's biggest fan, but she couldn't argue with what he'd said so far.

'As you no doubt already know, DCI Culverhouse is

on extended leave. How long that leave will be extended I don't know, but in his absence — which may very well be permanent — we're going to have to work together as a professional unit. That's going to mean doing things a little differently.'

Wendy noticed Steve Wing and Frank Vine exchange a glance with each other.

'Firstly, the practice of going off and doing your own thing and just updating everyone at the morning briefing if you feel like it is going to stop. All operational decisions, changes and manoeuvres *must* be ratified by your senior investigating officer — me. There will be no more role confusion. We will be organised in the same manner as any other CID department. The senior investigating officer — me — will remain here and oversee the investigation and not go gallivanting off and doing the legwork. I will be the eyes and ears of this operation. The hierarchy of ranks will be adhered to. That means that Detective Sergeants Knight, Wing and Vine will be given specific areas of the investigation to be getting on with. Detective Constables will work under the Sergeants.'

'Sir, we only have one Detective Constable at the moment,' Steve Wing said, gesturing to Debbie Weston.

'I'm aware of that, DS Wing,' Pope replied. 'And I'm currently liaising with my interim replacement at HQ to see if they can release a couple of constables to come and assist us. But of course I can't go putting any pressure on my interim replacement to do anything, because he's in charge there now.' He stopped talking for a moment and looked at each of the officers in the incident room, making sure the subtext of his message was hammered home. 'Each of you will be expected to write a written report of your day's activities at the end of each day and have it on my desk before you go home. Any external visits must be logged, and all interviews, whether internal or external, should have their audio recorded as well as notes taken.'

'Wait a second,' Frank Vine said. 'Audio recorded? You want us to carry tape recorders around with us now?'

'Not tape recorders,' Pope replied. 'Dictaphones. It's something I introduced at Milton House and it works very well. Gives us an extra layer of evidence in court. Not that our written notes aren't taken seriously, but it's kind of hard for a jury to ignore a recorded conversation, if you see what I mean.'

Wendy couldn't argue with that, but she found herself feeling slightly uneasy. As far as ethical and progressive policing went, she was certainly on the same side of the fence as Malcolm Pope, but she had to admit that recording external interviews didn't quite sit right with her. People always tended to act differently when they were being filmed or recorded and the occasional off-the-record remarks or conversations would stop dead, which could make life far more difficult for them.

Malcolm Pope smiled. 'Needless to say there'll have to

be some more changes if we're going to get results quickly, but I think that'll do for now. If anyone needs me, I'll be in my new office on the third floor.'

Frank Vine raised an eyebrow. 'You not joining us in here, then? The guv always used to sit—'

'Like I said, Detective Sergeant Vine. Things are going to have to change.'

Malcolm Pope exited the room and headed in the direction of the lift. The incident room remained silent for a few moments before a chuckling Steve Wing broke the deadlock.

'Here, Frank. Mate said to me the other day, "Do you use your dictaphone?" I said, "No, I use my fingers like everyone else."'

Frank allowed himself a titter before getting back to the topic in hand.

'What was all that about then? Who does he think he is?'

'He's our new SIO, Frank. And I think he's got some pretty valid points,' Debbie Weston said.

'Are you having a laugh?' Frank replied, raising his voice. 'How can you be happy about it? As things stand, you're the only DC so you're left as the poor lackey doing our leg work.'

'I'm fine with that. I actually quite like the menial work.'

'Sod that,' Steve said. 'If I wanted menial work I'd've

got myself a job as a secretary. Reckon I'd look good in a skirt, Frank?'

'About as good as you look in anything. So no. Listen, if Malcolm Pope's gonna sit there and think he can change all the good work we've done over the years just because the guv's away, he's got another thing coming.'

Wendy shook her head and decided to take charge of the situation. 'We've not got much choice. The best thing we can do is get our heads down and get on with it. With any luck, the guv'll be back at work before long. We'll have trouble keeping him away, you know that.'

The other officers nodded, but looked far from convinced.

## 15

Wendy knew Jack Culverhouse needed help. That much was obvious. The culture changes in the police over the past couple of decades had really shaken up some of the old school officers like Culverhouse. He hadn't been in the force long when things started changing, but he was a stubborn git and he'd only ever joined because of what the police force was, and not what it was becoming. If he'd seen the changes on the horizon, it was doubtful he'd have ever joined in the first place, she thought.

He used to speak fondly of officers he'd worked with when he first joined the force. One, Jack Taylor, had been the DI when Culverhouse was a fresh-faced young PC trying to worm his way into CID. Taylor had been a corrupt bastard at best, but he knew what it took to get results and he was very much of the old school.

She'd also heard Culverhouse talk about an officer

named Robin Grundy, who'd retired a couple of years before she joined the force. It was Grundy who Culverhouse had taken over from as DCI at Mildenheath, with Grundy having privately chosen him as his successor a few years previously. That was the way things were then, and the vast majority of it had changed enormously since. There were a few remnants of the old school remaining, but they'd largely been marginalised.

Charles Hawes, the Chief Constable, was a man trying to be a friend to everyone, doing his best to please the elected Police and Crime Commissioner and sucking up to those who espoused the new way of doing things as well as keeping more than one leg in with the old school. Although he'd have called himself a diplomat, others thought he was weak and on the fence.

Culverhouse had told Wendy about how Jack Taylor had thrown his life away, hitting the bottle big time after an off-duty incident saw him having to resign from the force. She could certainly see the parallels with Culverhouse's current situation and, as much as he frustrated her, she simply couldn't allow herself to watch him go the same way as Jack Taylor.

Robin Grundy, on the other hand, had left Mildenheath CID all those years ago with his head held relatively high. He'd gone on to set up his own private investigation agency and had done fairly well for a few years before retiring completely and preferring to tend his garden and allotment instead. Every officer had to retire at some point, and Wendy would far rather Culverhouse went the way of Robin Grundy and enjoyed a few years on his allotment than going out how Jack Taylor did, lying in a gutter with only a bottle of whisky for comfort.

She'd arranged to meet Grundy at his home in Mareham, a small village four or five miles outside Mildenheath with a number of very big houses. When she finally found his house, she wondered if perhaps she'd ever live in a place like this. If she made DCI, she might stand a chance. As things stood right now, she'd be more than happy to just have one of the two cars he had proudly parked on his huge gravel drive — an E-class Mercedes and a new Jaguar.

She walked up to the front door and rang the doorbell, waiting for him to answer. He was still fairly young — probably only in his late sixties, Wendy thought, doing the maths — and by what she could see now he looked even younger. Police work didn't usually age a man well, but Robin Grundy had been the exception.

'DS Knight, I presume?' he said, smiling as he held the door open and beckoned her through. The hallway was light and airy, with a lot of wooden furniture and white paint. She followed Grundy through to the living room — one of a couple, she presumed — which had two low-backed sofas arranged around a large flat-screen TV on the far wall. They sat down on a sofa each.

'Sorry, I should have offered you a drink. Would you like a cup of tea?' Grundy said.

'I'm fine, thanks anyway,' Wendy replied. 'I just wondered if I could perhaps talk to you on a personal level. As one police officer to a former police officer, but not officially, if you see what I mean.'

Grundy smiled. 'Personal advice?'

'Sort of,' Wendy replied.

'Don't worry, I know exactly what you mean. The job's a cunt, right?'

Wendy tried not to look shocked at this seemingly well-to-do man's vulgar use of language, remembering he was very much from the same school of policing as Jack Culverhouse.

'Well, it's alright,' she said. 'I'm doing okay. There's someone else we have in common who isn't doing so well, though.'

'Jack Culverhouse?' Grundy said. 'Yes, I could've seen that coming. Especially after the Ripper stuff recently. He's been on a hiding to nothing since his wife left.'

'You knew about that?' Wendy asked.

'Oh yes. We were fairly close, Jack and I. Drifted apart somewhat recently, though. Happens a lot in that job. You go from month to month without realising you haven't spoken to anyone who isn't an officer, a crim or a nark. It takes over.'

It was Wendy's turn to smile. 'Tell me about it,' she

said. 'I don't know if you've heard, but he's on leave at the moment.'

Grundy's eyebrows rose. 'I hadn't. But then again there's no reason why I would've done. Voluntary or not?'

'Not entirely,' Wendy said. 'He's been a little less choosy with his words and actions recently and the upper echelons have become a lot more fussy. There's been a bit of crossover between those two things, see. Long story short, Hawes thought it would be a good idea if he took some time away.'

'Hawes going soft in his old age, is he?' Grundy asked.

'Something like that. Problem is, Jack's hit the bottle now. He's a cynical old bastard anyway, but there's just no getting through to him at all at the moment. He won't take any help and seems to be quite happy to just throw it all away.'

Grundy tapped out a rhythm on the arm of the sofa before he spoke. 'It was bound to happen eventually. Rock bottom, they call it. Most officers have been there at some point. You start to wonder what it's all about. You ask yourself why you bother. The biggest attraction is in self-destruction. I've seen it happen so many times.'

Wendy could see that Grundy had had some personal experience of this. He didn't need to say it; she could just tell. 'But what can I do to help him?'

Grundy raised his eyebrows and shook his head. 'Not an awful lot, unfortunately. He needs to help himself.

Easier said than done, I know, but that's the only way. The thing is, Wendy — can I call you Wendy? — he needs to feel needed. All officers do. That's why we do the job, because we want to help people who need us. We want to do a public service. When things change at a higher level in the police force, sometimes it feels like those changes are out of your control. With someone like Jack, whose way of doing things is so at odds with the bigwigs, that's likely to be amplified. He probably feels he's being squeezed out slowly and this whole being put on leave thing just proves that. You need to prove him wrong, prove that he's needed. Can you call on him for something?'

Wendy snorted. 'Already tried that. It was him taking a stand and leading from the front — or not, as the case may be — that got him into this mess in the first place. I can't go into the details, but there have been things going on which he's been... Let's just say he was reluctant to investigate as fully as he should've been.'

'I see,' Grundy said, raising his eyebrows again. 'Sweeping the dirt under the carpet, eh? Nothing new as far as I'm concerned, but I appreciate things have changed a lot in recent years.'

'You can say that again,' Wendy said, nodding. 'Unfortunately, Jack Culverhouse hasn't.'

## 16

Mildenheath's main church was a former abbey, an enormous twelfth-century stone building which stood in its own beautiful grounds, barely a stone's throw from the crossroads in the town centre but at the same time seeming a million miles away from it. It seemed completely oblivious to the urban sprawl which had sprung up around it, instead choosing to stand ignorantly amongst it, with just enough open space of its own to keep the modern day at arm's length.

The church had its own sombre history, being the place where royal divorces and the funerals of late medieval noblemen had occurred as well as having served as a safe house for royals during the English Civil War. Now, though, it was the site of the memorial service for PC Luke Baxter.

What struck Wendy the hardest was that life and daily

policing still went on despite the event. A number of officers were unable to make the service because of work.
Shifts had been moved to accommodate close friends and
colleagues of Luke's, but the cold fact of the matter was
that life went on.

On the other hand, a huge number of serving and
former police officers from across the country and beyond
had come to pay their respects to Luke, a man they'd never
known but with whom they'd shared a very personal bond;
a bond symbolised by a simple uniform, which every one of
them wore immaculately as they filed into the church.

Wendy recognised a number of familiar faces, not only
former colleagues and friends but also representatives from
the local and national press gathered outside the church,
who'd taken a great interest not only because of the death
of an on-duty police officer but the manner in which it had
happened, being shot by one of the most notorious serial
killers of recent times. She spotted Luke's aunt, Shirley,
and his older brother, Sam, at the front of the church,
speaking to the vicar. Thankfully, this was at least a safe
haven for them as the press had been explicitly told they
were not allowed inside the church as the service was for
friends, family and colleagues only.

A strange mixture of both sadness and pride swelled
up inside Wendy. Sadness at the loss of a fine young police
officer, but pride at the number of people who had turned
out to honour his memory. She chuckled inwardly as she

imagined the smug look on his face if he could've known how many people would come here for him. She wondered, briefly, if she would've received the same service had it been her who had died. The truth was it hadn't almost been her they were here for; it was Jack Culverhouse. What was going through his mind right now must've been ten times, a hundred times worse.

As the vicar began speaking, the words all rolled into one and Wendy realised she was barely listening to what was being said. She occasionally tuned back in before zoning out again, her mind preoccupied by her own thoughts and memories. She wondered if it was the same for the others at the service, too.

After a few minutes, Wendy heard the door at the entrance to the church open. She turned around to see Jack Culverhouse, not dressed in police uniform but in a white polo neck and dark chinos. He held a baseball cap in one hand and a pair of large sunglasses in the other. He wisely decided against making his way towards the pews and instead opted to skulk at the back of the church, out of sight.

As the congregation rose to sing Amazing Grace, Wendy saw him heading back towards the door. Thankful that she'd sat on the end of a row, she peeled off and headed in pursuit of him. As she got to the exit she could see Jack walking quickly across the gardens, the baseball cap and sunglasses having provided an effective disguise against the waiting press who were now in Wendy's way.

She knew the best tactic was to say absolutely nothing. Even saying 'No comment' or 'I'll be back in a minute and I'll speak to you then' was equivalent to opening up a friendly dialogue as far as the press were concerned, so she opted to keep quiet and instead followed Jack round towards the war memorial, masked from the church and the press throng by an ancient stone wall.

When she got to the war memorial, she found him stood, staring at it. She slowly made her way up to him and stood a few feet short.

'Heroes, these men. Every one of them,' he said, a slight slur coming through in his voice. 'Every single year in November we honour what they did for us. I do, too. I wear my poppy, I watch the Remembrance service and I come down here and lay a wreath. And do you know what? I didn't know a single one of the buggers. I wasn't even alive. My parents hadn't even met. But I still do it. And here we are, spending just one morning in church to honour the memory of a colleague, a friend, who until recently was living and breathing and laughing with us, and who sacrificed his life for mine. And can I even bring myself to sit at the back of a church and sing a couple of hymns for him? Can I fuck.' He sighed. 'What sort of man does that make me?'

Wendy walked closer to Jack and put an arm around

his shoulder, trying to avoid the strong, sweet smell of alcohol.

'It makes you a man with human emotions. A man who's struggling to come to terms with what's happened. And do you know what? That's absolutely fine. No-one's judging you.'

'I'm judging myself,' he said quietly, before the tears began to roll down his face and his shoulders began to heave.

Shortly after, Wendy was making her way back to the entrance to the church, not particularly keen herself on going back inside, but seeing it as preferable to hanging around with the photographers and reporters who were gathered outside.

Although they were all clamouring for a comment from Wendy as she passed through, the usually shy voice of Suzanne Corrigan made itself heard above the others; not because of its volume, but because of what she said.

'Detective Sergeant Knight, do you think the public's diminishing confidence in the police has led directly to the vigilante actions we've been seeing recently?'

Wendy tried to let no emotion show on her face as she pushed open the main door to the church and went inside.

## 17

He pulled up on the kerb on the opposite side of the road from the house, having changed the number plates on his Vauxhall Combo in a rural lay-by a couple of miles away. He knew it was away from any CCTV cameras and would allow him to get close enough to his target's house without being traceable.

The registration on the new plates matched that of an identical Vauxhall Combo owned by a van hire company on the outskirts of Birmingham. He'd looked at van hire companies' fleets online until he'd found one that matched. On the slight off-chance that someone mentioned to the police that they'd seen his van, the registration would lead them down a dead end.

Sure, they'd realise soon enough that false plates had been used. Then their first port of call would be to 'show plate' manufacturers on the internet — companies that had been set up with the public line that they were supplying number plates for shows and exhibitions and not to be used on the road, although they were used almost exclusively for people wanting to make their obscure, cheap personalised registration plate look more expensive than it actually was by illegally altering the spacing of letters and numbers.

They'd waste a good day or so phoning around those companies to see who'd made the registration, when in fact he'd made it using an old manual jig and roller set he'd bought four years earlier from a friend whose motor factors business had closed down, telling him he knew someone who wanted to buy it from him. He figured that four years was long enough for no-one to make the connection, particularly seeing as he'd be destroying the plates later tonight to remove all trace of the evidence anyway.

He straightened his tie, pulled the large winter jacket across his chest and opened the van door, stepping out into the bitter air. He crossed the quiet road and walked up the block-paved driveway of his target's house without glancing round. He knew it was better to act normally and confidently rather than trying to be too careful, which could just make him look suspicious.

He raised his finger and pressed the doorbell, hearing the electronic chime ring out inside the house. A few seconds later, a light came on behind the frosted glass panelling in the door and he heard the privacy chain being removed. A nice bonus, he thought.

The door opened and he recognised his target immediately. How valuable a tool Facebook could be.

'Terry Kendall?' he asked, trying to sound as confident and authoritative as possible.

'Yes,' the man replied, a slight look of confusion on his face.

'Detective Inspector Richard Thomson. Can I come in?'

'Why? What's it all about?' the man inside the house asked.

'I think it's better if we discuss the matter indoors.'

The man nodded and stood aside. 'Right, okay. Is something the matter?'

He said nothing and stepped inside the house, his right hand slipping inside his coat and removing the Taser from its holster. As the man closed the door and turned round to face him, he pulled the trigger, watching the man's body contort as he yelped in pain before collapsing to the floor.

Barely three minutes later, he was finished. He knew he'd been a little gratuitous with the last one and that he wouldn't always have as much time to get in and out. He certainly couldn't risk being caught too soon and having the police make out *he* was the criminal for doing their job for them, especially as they seemed to be completely incapable of doing it themselves.

Just as he was preparing to leave, he heard a car stopping outside and the engine being switched off. With this being a small cul-de-sac of just eight houses, he felt he had reason to be worried.

Those worries intensified as he heard the increasing sound of footsteps on the front path, followed by the chiming of the doorbell which rang through the house.

He held his breath and looked at the dead body of Terry Kendall laying just inside the living room, as if expecting it to call out and betray him.

Moments later, the bell rang again.

A muffled voice came from outside the front door.

'Terry, are you there? It's Kim.'

There was silence for a few moments. It was then that he saw the shadow move across the front of the bay window, darkening the net curtains as the figure moved between the window and the streetlight outside, which peered over the top of the tall hedges surrounding the driveway.

He had no choice but to move. He ducked back into the hallway and crouched down, moving back along the hallway and through into the dark kitchen. Putting a light on wasn't an option. He felt his way around and fumbled with the key in the back door, finally managing to get it open without making too much noise.

Within seconds he was clear of the fence and skirting

around the side of a neighbour's house, making his way silently back towards the road.

Judging by the lack of any kind of reaction from Terry Kendall's visitor, he could only presume the body wasn't visible from the front window. Thanking his lucky stars, he opened the door to his van, got in and drove away as calmly as he could.

## 18

Wendy had managed to hold off until the next morning. She didn't want to appear too desperate or for it to look like Suzanne Corrigan had hit on something, so she'd bitten her tongue and held on. It hadn't been easy, but often so much of policing was about biding your time and waiting for the right moment. Now, though, she needed answers so she picked up the phone and called Suzanne's direct number at the Mildenheath Gazette.

Suzanne Corrigan had been through the mill herself in recent times, and had been the intended final victim of the Mildenheath Ripper, coming face to face with him in her own home before the tussle that had ultimately cost PC Luke Baxter his life. She had been determined to not only put that behind her, though, but to ensure that the details had never been made known — not even to her colleagues on the Gazette. The official story had been purely that the incident had happened at a 'local address'. Saying any more would've either resulted in being catapulted to national fame — something Suzanne wasn't interested in — or being signed off work for the next six months. Again, not something she wanted.

Wendy knew all this, but there was no time for niceties; Wendy knew Suzanne could become flustered fairly easily and decided to jump straight in, hoping to catch her on the back foot.

'You made a comment at the memorial service yesterday about vigilantes. What did you mean?' Wendy asked.

There was a pause and Wendy heard Suzanne swallow before speaking.

'Just something we picked up on when we looked at the details surrounding the murder in Brunel Road the other day,' the reporter said meekly.

'What about it?' Wendy replied. 'We haven't released details of the victim's identity or anything to do with how he died. So what details are you talking about exactly?'

Suzanne seemed to gain some confidence from somewhere. 'It's our duty to investigate and report facts, Detective Sergeant. We weren't told anything was embargoed so we looked into the story ourselves.'

'Who did you speak to?' Wendy asked firmly.

'All sorts of people. Neighbours, friends, family—'

'He had no family,' Wendy interrupted.

'I know, we discovered that. And we also found out that Jeff Brelsford had received a police caution for sexual harassment of a sixteen-year-old girl.'

'And what led you to think that?' Wendy asked, not committing either way to accepting or denying what Suzanne had said.

'Is it true?' the reporter asked.

'Answer my question.'

'Mildenheath's a small town. People know people. Someone in the office knows someone who worked at the company when it happened.'

'Can you be a little more specific?' Wendy asked.

'I'm not going to reveal my sources, if that's what you're asking,' Suzanne replied.

Wendy decided to change the subject slightly. 'Has this "vigilante" nonsense been published anywhere?'

'Not yet.'

'And that's how it's going to remain. I don't want anything about Jeff Brelsford's caution published anywhere, alright? Because that's exactly what it was: a caution. He wasn't even tried, let alone convicted.'

'But he was placed on the sex offenders register, wasn't he?' Suzanne asked.

'The register is visible only to police and related law enforcement agencies. If you're claiming to have information from it, that's a very serious matter.'

'Like I said, people know people. It's a small town.'

Wendy had started to detect she was losing control of this conversation. 'I'm not going to keep going round in circles, Suzanne. I'm asking you nicely. Do not publish any details of this. Once it's all wrapped up, we'll speak about what's in the public interest.'

'And is this order coming from you or your senior investigating officer?' Suzanne asked. 'Because, let's face it, he has the final say.'

Wendy rubbed her temple and ground her teeth. 'Like you said, Suzanne, Mildenheath's a small town. If I were a crime reporter, I wouldn't want to rub the police up the wrong way. I'll call you when I have something for you.'

'Should I presume you haven't seen today's papers then?' Suzanne replied.

Without really listening, and before she could say anything else, Wendy had hung up the phone. She had tried not to sound rude, and she knew how valuable the press could be in helping to spread the word and gather information, but the last thing the investigation needed right now was for hysteria to break out on either side, either from sex offenders worried about vigilante attacks or local residents being up in arms about offenders being housed in their area.

Of course no-one wanted to live next to a sex offender out of choice, but the fact of the matter was that they had to live somewhere. The most serious offenders were moni-tored extremely closely, but from what Wendy could make out Jeff Brelsford was far from being one of the most serious offenders. His actions had been considered to constitute harassment, but it appeared to have been a one-off and had not resulted in prosecution or conviction. Why, then, had he been targeted? There were dozens of bigger targets in the local area if this truly was about vigilante action.

Every time that thought led Wendy towards the presumption that they could be wrong about Jeff Brelsford's murder being a vigilante killing, she kept coming back to the cold, hard facts: the signs of torture, the Taser to the genitals and the removal of said apparatus. Not exactly the hallmarks of a burglary gone wrong. Nothing, as far as they could see, had been taken from the house and it seemed that Jeff Brelsford had been targeted deliberately. In the absence of any other reason for someone wanting him dead, and due to the way he was killed, the only clear motive was a sexual revenge of some sort.

As she mulled this over, the door opened and Malcolm Pope strode in with all the confidence of a Wild West gunslinger.

'I've just had uniform on the phone,' he said. 'A district nurse called on one of her patients in Southbrook this morning. Alveston Close. She had no response last night or this morning, so she was worried and called the police. Uniform went in and found the owner dead in his living room.'

'Unless this is just a nice little story, I presume you're telling me because there's more to it,' Wendy said, her patience now running very thin.

'Oh yes. There's much more,' Malcolm Pope said, smiling. 'But how would Taser scarring and some detached genitals do for starters?'

19

Jack Culverhouse threw another newspaper on the coffee table and rested his head back against the sofa.

It was a hatchet job. The tabloids led with their pathetic *RIPPER COPPER HITS ROCK BOTTOM* and *HERO COP LOSES THE PLOT* headlines and the opinion pieces in the broadsheets ranged from *CULVER-HOUSE AFTERMATH LIFTS THE LID ON THE DARK SIDE OF POLICING* to *HARVEY RATBERGER ASKS: SHOULD WE INCREASE PSYCHOLOGICAL SUPPORT TO FRONTLINE POLICE?*

The disparity between the two types of newspaper was extraordinary. Anything with a red top was primarily interested in dramatising the fact that he'd been placed on leave (or 'sent home to sort his head out', as one particularly sensitive publication put it) as well as speculating on whether his current situation was purely a reflection on what had happened or if he'd actually been unstable at the time and had somehow caused Luke Baxter's death. Culverhouse had seen the extraordinary spin the press could put on non-stories a thousand times in his line of work, but this was something else.

The broadsheets and left-leaning newspapers seemed to be somewhat more sympathetic, sensibly looking at the causes and what could be done rather than trying to sensationalise a grown man's health struggles. They referred to previous famous cases of post-traumatic stress syndrome, which all of the papers — all of the ones that could spell it, anyway — were in agreement was what had happened to Jack Culverhouse.

To him, though, it didn't matter whether he had a medical condition or had 'gone off the rails' or 'cracked up'; the fact was that he was a man lost. Fortunately for him, the newspapers had dropped all the blame at the door of what had happened that night at Suzanne Corrigan's house. They had no inkling as to everything else that had affected his state of mind and he had no intention of telling them. It would only be a matter of time before they'd cotton on, though.

Every man had his limits. Even Jack Culverhouse. For years he'd enjoyed a reputation that involved being invincible, emotionless and able to take whatever shit his job and his life threw at him. As far as he was aware, the majority of his colleagues weren't aware he'd even been married, never mind that his wife had left him out of the blue and taken their young daughter with her.

Oddly enough, it wasn't Helen's disappearance that hurt the most. Even he had to admit that he'd neglected her and his daughter, Emily, who he'd let down in favour of his job and had barely seen in her waking hours up until the day they upped and left. What had hurt the most was Helen returning without Emily and telling him in no uncertain terms that Emily didn't want to see him.

There was no way she could have formed that opinion on her own. She was too young when they left. Any kind of animosity had to come, at best, through her not under-standing what had been going on at that time or, at worst, through Helen poisoning her mind from an early age. He knew which one he thought was true. Helen was pure poison.

The only person who knew that Helen had recently — briefly — returned was Wendy Knight. He wasn't a man who trusted easily, but he knew he could trust Wendy with things like that. Even so, he had no intention of telling her everything that was going through his mind. That would be far too dangerous.

Luke's death had been the straw that had broken the camel's back. He hadn't known it at the time, but he had been perilously close to cracking for a while. Would he have stopped and taken a break even if he had known it? He very much doubted it. Taking time off wasn't something Jack Culverhouse did, and even now he was quite sure it was making things worse instead of better. The amount of scotch he was drinking was testament to that. Besides which, there was only so much *Judge Rinder* a man could watch.

The truth was, if he wasn't working he was lost. He'd quickly come to realise that Mildenheath CID was his *raison d'etre*. That could now all be lost to history, though. The thought of retirement had petrified him and it was something he'd never entertained as a plan. He knew that he'd be pensioned off at some point, but in his mind even planning for the event would be tantamount to wishing it into existence. It wasn't a thought he could bear; just having been away from the job for a matter of days was already killing him.

If it had been a simple case of being signed off sick, he would've ignored it and gone straight back to work, dealing with it the only way he knew how. This time, though, it was different. This time he wasn't in control. He had been placed on official leave and couldn't go back to work if he wanted to. The only way back was to show that he was back to normal, or as normal as he'd ever been.

That was easier said than done. There was no way he could do it by himself, and there was no-one he could call on for help. The only person who had ever been able to deal with Jack Culverhouse was Jack Culverhouse.

## 20

The journey to Southbrook took them a shade under fifteen minutes. The village was a busy one, nestled by the side of the motorway and famous only for its service station as well as being on one of the main arterial routes through the county that didn't involve motorways or dual carriageways.

Alveston Close was tucked away neatly on the quieter side of the village away from the main drag, and it seemed unlikely to Wendy that Terry Kendall and Jeff Brelsford would have had much in common. That said, they certainly had one thing in common: they were both dead. That and they'd both been killed in a remarkably similar manner, very possibly by the same person.

Wendy noticed the tall hedge that surrounded the front of the property, effectively masking it from prying eyes but also providing fantastic protection for burglars.

And murderers. One notable absence was the gathering crowd of neighbours and passers-by that had been present outside Jeff Brelsford's house. There was no such interest here. Probably all at work, she thought. Hardly the sort of place people would just be wandering past, either.

She spotted Janet Grey's car parked a little further along the road. It always amazed her how the pathologist could manage to get to any scene of a crime quicker than she could. She thought she must have some sort of in-built radar. It made sense that you'd pick up some sort of nose for death after a few years.

She smiled at the uniformed officer standing guard at the end of the driveway as she walked towards the door. The block paving looked lovely, she thought, but gravel might've been a little more effective at drawing attention to any unwanted visitors. Bit late for that now.

The front door was ajar and she let herself in, heading in the direction of the living room. It was the smell that hit her first. Any time a body had lain undiscovered for more than a few hours, the smell would be almost unbearable. No amount of experience in seeing dead bodies could desensitise you to that stench, but Janet Grey seemed to be coping admirably. Then again, Wendy thought, she was practically superhuman.

'Ah, good morning,' Dr Grey said in her usual chirpy manner. 'Action Man not come with you?'

'No, he's decided to delegate,' Wendy replied. 'Apparently an eight hundred word report is just as good as coming out to see it for himself.'

'Don't tell Jack,' the pathologist replied, pulling a few strands of hair out of Terry Kendall's head with a pair of tweezers. 'He'll go spare.'

Wendy smiled. 'I think he's probably got a fair idea as to what's going on in his absence. So what's the lowdown?'

'Seventy-three-year-old male, might as well be twice that. All sorts of medical conditions according to the district nurse who found him. She came last night to change a dressing and top up his medication but there was no answer. Not a rare occurrence, apparently, so she left it until the morning as there wasn't anything urgent. When she got no response again this morning she rang the police.'

'How long's he been dead?' Wendy asked.

'Difficult to say exactly until I'm back at the lab, but it's at least eleven hours if that thermometer on the wall's right.'

Wendy looked at the thermometer. 21 degrees celsius. She knew from past experience that a dead body would cool from 37.5 degrees at a rate of 1.5 degrees an hour until it reached ambient temperature.

'No longer than twenty-four hours, though, as rigor's not worn off yet, even in the small joints. Besides which, the nurse saw him alive and well this time yesterday. Best I can say is that it was probably, possibly, between four o'clock yesterday afternoon and eleven last night.'

'Brilliant, thanks Janet. Where's the nurse who found him?'

'She's outside in the van taking advantage of the obligatory mug of sweet tea. More than I get, and I've got to sit here poking the thing.'

'Always good to see someone who loves their job,' Wendy said, trying to play the pathologist at her own cynical game. 'What do we know about the IP?' she asked the uniformed constable.

'His name was Terry Kendall according to the nurse. She confirmed it was him. Retired schoolteacher, apparently.'

'What about family?' Wendy asked.

'None to speak of. He was an only child, never married and his parents are long gone, obviously.'

'I'd guessed that bit,' Wendy replied. 'How often does the nurse come?'

'Every morning and evening between nine and ten,' the officer replied. 'He's got an open wound on his back from some surgery that didn't heal properly, so she came to change the dressing twice a day and update his medication.'

'And everything was fine yesterday morning?'

'Well he wasn't dead, if that's what you mean,' Janet Grey interrupted.

'The nurse said she didn't spot anything wrong,' the officer said. 'Think that's why it came as a bit of a shock when she found him this morning. She's used to patients dying between visits, but Mr Kendall wasn't exactly at death's door. He just didn't have anyone around who could change his dressing and he couldn't get to his GP twice a day.'

Wendy nodded and let the officer leave.

Janet Grey shook her head. 'Got to say, Wendy, I'd be looking a bit deeper into this. Especially considering the patterns and connection with the way that Brelsford chap went. You know I'm not one to theorise,' she said, a moment before Wendy raised her eyebrow, 'but it looks to me like you might be after the same person here too.'

'Yes,' Wendy said, swallowing. 'That's what I'm worried about.'

## 21

He hammered his fist into the side of his own head. How could he be so fucking *stupid*? Having to go out the back door and vault the fence was one thing, but even so he shouldn't have got flustered and left the laptop.

He had no option; he couldn't go back. Rule number one, that: Never return to the scene of the crime. He knew, though, that one of the first things the police would do would be to look through Terry Kendall's laptop. And then what? It was entirely — very — possible that they'd find something that led back to him.

He'd been extraordinarily careful to hide his own identity, emailing only when connected to a VPN and via TOR where possible. Even so, he wasn't fully confident. You never knew these days how much the police could do, whether they'd be able to somehow get the data they needed to trace him. He was willing to bet that if he'd been the victim of a crime they'd very quickly hold their hands up and say there was nothing they could do because the other person had connected via a proxy server. It was sod's law, though, that they'd throw their biggest tech geeks at this one.

No, he had to think calmly and rationally. Why would they? They'd have to be pretty damn sure that there was something worth looking for. He tried to rack his brains to think what would be there. Terry Kendall had come unstuck after clicking on one of his links without being behind his usual cover of a VPN. It was possible that the page would still be in his browser history, but he doubted it. Someone with the perverted mind that he had would've cleared his browser history pretty frequently. In any case, the page couldn't be linked to him even if he hadn't.

Terry Kendall was one of those people who'd read a web page or two about computer security but really didn't have a clue about it. He thought he knew more than he actually did. That was a godsend when it came to trying to find out his identity while he was known only as JackRabbit12, but could cause a problem now. The only hope was that the police wouldn't look too deeply and wouldn't think anything of finding the TOR browser on Terry Kendall's laptop.

He had to remind himself that they'd have no real reason to go through his laptop in such detail. Why would they prioritise it as a clue? They'd be looking at his emails to see if he'd mentioned arguments or disagreements with anyone, and that could possibly lead them to the link he'd sent Terry which eventually divulged his IP address. He figured it was unlikely Terry would've kept that, though.

It was also pretty unlikely that that email account would've been his main or only account. Surely he wouldn't have been that stupid, would he? No. It was unthinkable.

Fortunately for him, the TOR browser didn't store users' browsing histories, so he was fairly confident that the police wouldn't be led to the forum. In the meantime, he had only one option.

Hands shaking as he did so, he entered the administration panel on the forum and locked it down to be accessible only to the user accounts he'd invited, making sure he also disabled JackRabbit12's account, just on the off-chance the police did make a connection and try accessing the forum through Terry Kendall's laptop.

As of now, the only people who'd be able to access the forum were him and his remaining targets.

## 22

The back of a police van wasn't the most comfortable place to conduct an interview, but Wendy had been in worse places. Kim Kelliher, the district nurse, seemed visibly shocked despite having seen her fair share of dead bodies in her time.

'It was the way he was lying there. I've never seen a murdered body before. Most people just die in their sleep or something,' she said, her voice quivering.

'Do you know any of his friends or family at all? Did he mention anybody else?' Wendy asked.

'No, no-one. He never married, I know that much. And he mentioned a while back that he had no brothers or sisters. He used to be a teacher, he said. On the coast somewhere. He did say where, but I can't remember.'

It struck Wendy as a little odd that someone would

spend their life working near the coast and choose to retire to Southbrook. It was usually the other way round.

'Did he seem agitated at all recently? Like he might have known he was under some sort of threat? Or that someone wanted him dead?'

'No, not at all. He was always really cheery considering the amount of pain he was in. The hospital really made a mess of his operation and it's never healed properly. That's the problem with back surgery sometimes.'

'There was no indication at all that anything was wrong?' Wendy asked, leaning in towards Kim. 'Only the injuries that killed him were pretty brutal. Whoever did this was pretty hell-bent on killing him.'

'No, nothing. Couldn't it have been a burglar or something? Perhaps he disturbed them.'

'I doubt it,' Wendy said. 'Nothing seems to have been taken, plus Terry was seventy-three. You wouldn't need that level of violence to subdue him. Whoever did it wanted to inflict real pain.'

Kim looked away, as if doing so would make everything stop. As Wendy went to speak again, the constable she'd been speaking to earlier knocked on the door of the van.

'Sarge, have you got a sec? We've found something.'

Wendy put a placating hand on Kim's shoulder and hopped out of the van.

'What is it?'

'The back door from the kitchen was unlocked, which

isn't all that strange, but there are footprints in the flower bed. The mud was pretty damp and soft, fortunately for us, so forensics should be able to get a decent cast. They say it looks like whoever did it was running, based on the pressure points and the one that's scuffed up next to the fence. Speaking of which, there's mud stuck to the top of the fence. Looks as though our man was disturbed and bolted across the flower bed and over the fence.'

'Right. See if you can trace that mud any further,' Wendy said. She worked out the timings in her head. Janet Grey said that Terry Kendall had probably died between four in the afternoon and eleven at night. Kim Kelliher, the district nurse, had rung the doorbell at about nine-thirty in the evening. It could well be possible that it was she who had disturbed the killer. She decided she wouldn't tell her that just yet.

When she got back to the van, she poked her head round the door and tried not to show too much excitement or concern.

'Kim, I don't suppose you remember what cars or vehicles were parked up around here when you came last night do you?'

Kim paused for a moment before shaking her head. 'No. No, I don't, I'm afraid. Why?'

Wendy smiled as best she could. 'No matter.'

Blatant rudeness wasn't something Wendy handled well, so when she heard the door to the incident room open, only to look up and see Malcolm Pope beckoning her with his finger to follow him, she wasn't put in the cheeriest frame of mind.

Pope stood in the corridor with his hands on his hips.

'What's the latest on this second body?' he asked, without even so much as saying hello.

Wendy tried not to let her annoyance show.

'You'll have all the necessary information in the end-of-day report, sir.'

'I'd like an update now, please,' Pope replied firmly.

'As well as a report at the end of the day?' Wendy asked, folding her arms.

Pope narrowed his eyes. 'Do I detect a slight hint of animosity, Detective Sergeant Knight?'

Wendy stood and looked at him for a couple of seconds before changing the subject. 'A man was found dead in his house in Southbrook. Similar MO to the Jeff Brelsford killing. We're speaking to neighbours and assessing the evidence as we speak.'

'How similar?'

'Similar enough for us to be concerned,' Wendy replied.

'Taser?'

'Yes. And throat lacerations.'

'Do we have a positive ID on the deceased?' Pope asked.

Wendy thought for a moment. 'No, not yet,' she lied. She needed to keep some things to herself, especially considering the delicate political situation at Mildenheath CID.

Pope looked at her and nodded. She thought for a moment that perhaps he had already spoken to someone else and been given the details, but she thought it unlikely. 'And what leads are you following up?' he asked.

Wendy clenched her teeth. 'Sir, with respect, if you want a report on your desk at the end of the day from each of us and you want us to be able to dedicate enough time to investigating these cases, I really can't stand around giving you the same information verbally as well. Unless, of course, I'm going to be excused from having to write the report if you've already been told verbally.' She quickly realised that hadn't sounded half as professional as she'd hoped it would. Although she'd been feeling more confident in her role recently, she knew that a pasting from Pope right now would put her firmly on the back foot.

Malcolm Pope straightened his back. 'DS Knight, I know you had a cushy little number while DCI Culverhouse was leading this unit, but you have to accept that things have to be done a certain way. These aren't my rules. I think I should remind you of that. This is the way policing is done across the country, and I don't appreciate you using that tone with me.'

Wendy had never considered herself one to defend Jack Culverhouse, but right now she wished he was back running the team instead of Malcolm Pope. She'd been espousing the same style of policing as Malcolm Pope for years, but was quickly starting to realise that it was going to end up placing more restrictions on the investigation than Culverhouse's laissez-faire approach to things. At Milton House, it might be feasible, but then again their investigation teams were much, much larger. She was now starting to see that this was probably because at least half of them were dedicated purely to paperwork. The considerably smaller CID team at Mildenheath had managed to cope admirably over the years owing to its efficiency and focus on pure policing.

'You do realise, don't you, that there are plans afoot to

amalgamate Mildenheath CID into Milton House?' Pope said, a wry smile breaking across his face.

'I think a few of us had guessed that may be the case,' Wendy said, giving him her own sarcastic smirk.

'And when that happens you're going to be working for me permanently, so you're going to have to get used to this.'

Wendy decided she was going to stand her ground. 'You seem to be assuming that it's actually going to happen,' she said. 'You do know this isn't anything new, right? They've been trying to move us up there for years. The PCC's been getting his knickers in a twist about it ever since he got elected, but you know what he said after the Ripper case. We're going nowhere.'

Pope smiled again. 'He didn't say that, though, did he? He said the move was on hold. Holds are temporary.'

'Are we getting into semantics now?' Wendy said, laughing. 'We both know what it meant. There's no way he'd get away with upsetting the apple cart after a result like that.'

'A result like what? Letting four innocent people get murdered, then putting the local news reporter in mortal danger and having a serving police officer killed in the process of saving her life? Oh yes, what a result.'

'The killer was caught,' Wendy said firmly. 'In my book, that's a result.'

Pope shook his head. 'But at what cost? If you think

that investigation was a success, you're barking. It was a failure and you know it.'

'Not according to the Chief Constable, it wasn't. And as far as I'm concerned, that's all that matters. As long as he's around, there's no way in hell you'll get away with speaking to people the way you do and there's about as much chance of us being shipped off to Milton House to fill in paperwork with you and your pen-pushing chums.' Even as she spoke, Wendy was shocked at how much she sounded like Jack Culverhouse.

Pope laughed. 'You're right, yes. As long as he's around, DS Knight. As long as he's around.' He shook his head, laughed again and headed off in the direction of the lift.

## 24

Frank Vine looked proud as punch as he plonked his note-book down on Wendy's desk.

'Look at that,' he said. 'What do you make of that?'

Wendy squinted and cocked her head sideways as she looked at the notepad. 'Uh, I'm not sure. My years of experience as a detective would probably say that a spider got into your ink pot then walked around on your notepad for a bit.'

'Cheeky bitch,' Frank said, snatching the notepad back. 'Do you want me to decipher for you?'

'I wouldn't mind.'

'Right, well basically I've just heard back from Liz Prior in forensics. They've taken casts of the footprints found in Terry Kendall's back garden. They're pretty sure there was only one person, and he was running pretty quickly from the back door in the kitchen to the fence.

They reckon he jumped up at the fence mid-stride as there are some scuff marks on the wood. He then clambered up onto the top of it, leaving some mud from the flowerbed on the top, landed on the other side and made his way back round the neighbours' garden to the road.'

'Where did he go from there?' Wendy asked.

'They're not sure. There were traces of mud as far as the road, but the roadsweepers were round about half an hour before the district nurse found him dead. Sod's bloody law.'

'And nothing on the pavement on the other side of the road?' Wendy asked.

'Nope, nothing. Which is a bit weird in itself. They reckon he either ran up the road itself or got into a car that was parked outside.'

Wendy fancied the latter to be more likely. 'And what about the prints? Did they identify the shoes?'

'Not yet, and they don't fancy their chances. The chap wasn't wearing trainers, by all accounts. Flat bottomed, leather soles. Could be absolutely anything. They're doing their best, though. But get this. We've reviewed the CCTV from the streets near Jeff Brelsford's and Terry Kendall's homes. A neighbour's private CCTV shows a small white van heading in the direction of Terry Kendall's house and parking up nearby on the night he was killed. It's there for about five minutes. Looks almost identical to another van seen passing a camera on Mildenheath High Street in the direction of Jeff Brelsford's house a few minutes before the bloke across the road says he saw a guy in a suit. Quarter of an hour later, the same van heads back in the other direction past the same camera. We lose it on the south side of town, heading out towards the motorway, but the motorway cameras didn't pick it up, so it's probably gone off into the country lanes somewhere.'

'Christ. Did you get a registration?'

'Yep. And it matches a white Vauxhall Combo registered to a van hire company in Birmingham called Bower & Sons. Only problem is, that van's sat on their forecourt and has been for the past week and a half. No-one's hired it in that time and they say it's not left the West Midlands in the last couple of months, so it wasn't that van that was seen in town.'

'What, so someone's cloned the number plate?'

'Seems like it. Someone who managed to find out that there was a van of exactly the same type somewhere in the country with this number plate on it.'

'Someone who'd hired it before?'

'Possibly, although it's fairly new and has only been hired out six times. It's never been south of Coventry, apparently. But get this. I was on their website trying to find their phone number, and they've got listings of all their vans for hire. With pictures. Showing the number plates. To be honest, that's probably what I would've done too. Not difficult these days what with the internet and everything. Only tricky bit would be getting the physical plates made up, but that's far from impossible.'

'That sounds good enough for me, Frank. Get the company to get onto their web hosts and get the server logs. If we can get a list of people who've looked at that page, we can narrow it down to our man.'

Frank grinned from ear to ear. 'Looks like we might have our man!'

## 25

Suzanne Corrigan had been feeling stronger every day. She was a naturally shy person, but keen to ensure that she got the right story for her paper. Coming face to face with the Mildenheath Ripper had taught her a lot about life, and she was finding the mundane things far less daunting after that particular ordeal.

For one thing, she'd learnt that life was too short. Although she'd always tried to keep her moral compass in check — something which was very difficult in the world of journalism — she now understood the sanctity of life and saw the damage that could easily be done. Even so, she didn't feel she was prying by trying to find out exactly what was going on in the world of Jack Culverhouse.

He'd been taking leave from work, that much she knew. That wasn't particularly surprising, though, after the time he'd been having of it recently. Mildenheath CID hadn't exactly been the quietest of police departments in the last few years. As far as she could see, though, there seemed to be more to it. Signs and signals had been coming her way as a result of a dogged press gang who were keen to milk as much from the Mildenheath Ripper story as they could, combined with Jack Culverhouse's propensity to not give a shit. The fact that he seemed to be going off the rails, then, was fairly easy to ascertain.

What was most intriguing, though, was the secrecy that had surrounded the body found in Southbrook. It was a murder; she knew that much due to the fact that CID had attended the scene and forensics were working all hours combing the house for clues. What had really piqued her interest, though, was just how much secrecy was being placed on it all.

She prided herself on having a good relationship with the police — she deemed that vital to the job — but they'd gone completely cold on her with this one. She told herself that could be down to any number of things: the new DCI running the show while Culverhouse was on leave or even her stupid decision to try and put Wendy Knight on the spot about Jeff Brelsford's killer having murdered him in some sort of vigilante attack.

Perhaps that wasn't such a stupid comment, though. In light of recent developments she could actually have been much closer to the truth than she'd known. What if the reason the police were reluctant to release any information on the Southbrook death was because they thought the same person had killed both people? Her only way of finding out was to discover who the dead body in Southbrook was and to do a bit of digging around to find out some connections, but that made her uneasy.

She didn't want to compromise her good relationship with the police — that was never a good idea for a local crime reporter — and her sense of morality kept telling her she had to do things the proper, right way. Sometimes, though, that moral compass seemed to suffer from magnetic interference.

Deciding to bite the bullet, she picked up the phone before she could even think of what she was going to say and dialled Wendy Knight's number. After four rings, the phone was answered. She could tell straightaway that DS Knight wasn't massively keen on speaking to her. Regardless, she decided the best move was to get straight to the point.

The first thing she noted was that Wendy seemed somewhat distracted as she answered the phone. Once Suzanne had introduced herself, though, she soon had her attention.

'I just wanted to ask you a couple of questions,' she said. 'It's related to what I asked you the other day at the memorial service.'

There was a short pause before Wendy spoke. 'What about it?'

'Are you able to tell me if there's any link between the two deaths?'

'That's something we're investigating at the moment,' Wendy said. 'But I certainly would not suggest speculating about it. If you want anything further, you'll have to speak to the senior investigating officer.'

Nice move, Suzanne thought. Put the pressure on Malcolm Pope instead. Even though she didn't work for the police, the office politics at Mildenheath CID were all too familiar to her by now. 'Are you able to give me any more information on the body discovered in Southbrook?' she asked. 'Only it seems to have been kept rather quiet. I wondered why that was.'

Wendy's response was professional and noncommittal. 'We'll be making an announcement in due course if we deem it prudent. And I don't want any of this going into any newspaper articles, alright? Not until the DCI has cleared it for public release.'

'I understand,' Suzanne said. 'Onto something else, you know there's a public interest in Jack Culverhouse at the moment, right? Especially after the Ripper case. I just wondered how he was getting on. I hear he's on leave.'

'He's had a very busy couple of years,' Wendy said. 'He's not had so much as a holiday in God knows how long, so I think we can safely say he deserves a rest.'

'So it was voluntary then?' Suzanne asked, putting Wendy on the spot.

Wendy said nothing for a few moments.

'Has he been subject to disciplinary action?' Suzanne said, probing further.

Wendy still said nothing. She was trying to think how to word her response, but nothing was coming to mind.

'DS Knight, I think the public have a right to know whether or not—'

'No, Suzanne, they do not,' Wendy replied, suddenly finding her voice. 'What the public do have a right to know, however, is how and why you've been digging up information about murder victims' employment histories.'

'I already told you,' Suzanne said. 'It's a small town.'

Wendy was furious now. 'No, Suzanne, that's bullshit. You can't just get away with dodging my questions with vague answers and demanding that I answer everything of yours. I'm afraid it doesn't work like that. If you want anything — *anything* — more out of me on this case and any others, apart from an official injunction stopping you from publishing a word, then you're going to have to tell me where that information came from.'

Wendy knew she was playing with fire. She needed the press as much as the press needed the police, but Suzanne didn't have to know that. The threat of an injunction should still have its desired effect, she thought. What she couldn't risk was having someone spreading their own theories around Mildenheath about who may or may not have committed a sexual offence at some point in their life.

Not while there was a vigilante roaming the streets, anyway.

'The connection is me,' Suzanne said finally. 'My best friend is the older sister of Katie McCourt.'

'Older sister?' Wendy asked, trying to do the maths. Fortunately for her, Suzanne had picked up on it.

'Yeah, she's nine and a half years older than Katie. We shared a flat together when I first came to live here from Cardiff. I wanted to get into journalism but most papers want degrees or qualifications, which I don't have. The Mildenheath Gazette was one of the only ones that didn't need them.'

That didn't surprise Wendy in the slightest. The Gazette didn't exactly have a reputation for quality and accuracy.

'That's how I ended up here,' Suzanne continued. 'I wanted to get out of Cardiff anyway and liked the idea of being nearer London, so Mildenheath seemed ideal. It took me a little while to get onto the Gazette, but I looked online for a flat and found a site where people advertise for flatmates. That's where I found Anna's advert. She wanted to flat-share with a woman of a similar age, so I got in touch.'

'And she just decided to tell you her younger sister was sexually molested by Jeff Brelsford?' Wendy asked.

'No, of course not. It wasn't like that. I was still working as a junior, writing up the crap about lost dogs, village fêtes and all that sort of stuff. You know, the articles that are attributed to "Gazette Reporter". The crime reporter job hadn't come up yet. Anna came home one day and was devastated. We opened a bottle of wine and she told me what had happened.'

'But this was a year ago,' Wendy said. 'You mean to say you just remembered it all and joined the dots?'

Suzanne let out an involuntary laugh. 'I have a memory for names. I don't often forget them.'

Wendy realised she needed to sit on this for a bit. If Suzanne Corrigan had a direct connection to Katie McCourt, she might have some extra insight into the family's real thoughts and feelings towards Jeff Brelsford.

'Can we meet?' Wendy said. 'Perhaps go and grab coffee somewhere. I think it'd be good to make sure we're both singing from the same hymn sheet so we can get along.'

'Sounds good to me,' Suzanne said, perhaps sensing the opportunity to gather some more information on the case. 'And then you can tell me all about Jack Culverhouse.'

## 26

Wendy's head was pounding more than it usually did. Probably just a tension headache, she told herself. Having to spend an extra hour or two each evening writing a report for Malcolm Pope probably didn't help. Sleep was hard to come by during an investigation as it was, and the extra stress she and the rest of the team were being put under wasn't going any way to making things better.

She'd always assumed that things might be better under a different DCI. Not that she ever wanted Culverhouse gone, but she had often wondered what would change if someone else were in charge. She quickly realised that, as with most things, neither extreme was the answer and the best way forward lay somewhere in the middle. Culverhouse's bull-in-a-china-shop approach was far from ideal and had its own drawbacks to say the least, but Malcolm Pope seemed to want to turn decent officers into pen-pushers. Some people didn't mind too much.

Debbie Weston, for example, had always been quite happy to do whatever needed to be done and wasn't fussed about furthering her own career. She was a thoroughly decent officer, but didn't have any airs or pretensions. Steve Wing and Frank Vine were similar in that respect but weren't exactly keen on the idea of being office-bound, especially as it added to their workload. Their favoured way forward was to get results by doing as little as possible.

She could see now why Jack Culverhouse was far from keen on Malcolm Pope. Their styles and ways of working and managing a team were so far removed from each other that it would be completely impossible for them to work together. As far as Culverhouse was concerned, he'd been heading up the CID unit at Mildenheath for long enough to know what worked — and it usually did — but Pope clearly saw him as something of a dinosaur, a relic of the old way of doing policing and someone who was no longer relevant.

Tensions had come to a head during the hunt for the Mildenheath Ripper, with Pope claiming that the killer could've been caught sooner and more lives could've been saved. Publicly, Culverhouse disagreed vehemently and he'd been fortunate to have the support of the Chief Constable, who wasn't Malcolm Pope's biggest fan either. The fact that Culverhouse had been extremely reluctant to follow the Ripper line of the inquiry when it was first postulated had been hastily glossed over.

Focusing on the mistakes would've made no difference. Learning from things that went wrong was usually beneficial, but in the case of the Mildenheath Ripper it would have caused more harm than good. Besides which, the town was unlikely to experience another serial killer, wasn't it? Unfortunately for Wendy, she knew that serial killings required three or more murders by the same person. They had two on their hands already, and if their theory about the vigilante was right, there'd be more.

Another series of murders in Mildenheath would probably finish the CID unit off and result in it being amalgamated into Malcolm Pope's unit in Milton House. Jack Culverhouse's career would certainly be finished, and Wendy had seen what a temporary suspension had done to the man. Retirement would be the death of him.

A thought crossed her mind as to whether Malcolm Pope was being deliberately obstructive in the way he was temporarily running the unit. It'd be in his best interests, after all. Another perceived Mildenheath failure would mean he'd effectively run CID in the county. He had a glowing record at Milton House and one little blip now wouldn't blot his copy book in the slightest, especially as he could simply blame it on the old-fashioned way of working and the culture at Mildenheath, which he was convinced was bad for policing.

Her silence was broken by the arrival of DS Steve Wing, who entered the room with a beaming smile on his face.

'Got some big news on the Jeff Brelsford and Terry Kendall murders,' he said, standing proud as punch.

'Great,' Wendy replied, resting her head on her hand. 'DCI Pope's upstairs.'

'Nah. If it's not written on paper he's not interested, so sod him. I've come to you instead.'

Wendy smiled at this as Steve continued.

'We've found a connection between the killings. I mean, apart from them being practically identical, I mean. A connection between the victims. Remember how Jeff Brelsford was cautioned for sexual harassment? Well get this. The tech lads have been through Terry Kendall's laptop. Kiddy porn. Tons of the stuff.'

'Are you serious?' Wendy asked.

'Deadly. They reckon that's probably just the tip of the iceberg though. Apparently there was some secret browser or something on there which he could've used to access the more hardcore stuff and it wouldn't leave a trace. My question is if the stuff they've found is just the soft stuff, what the hell's he been hiding with the secret browser thing?'

'Jesus, he was a schoolteacher wasn't he?'

'Yep. Doesn't mean anything though. You'd be surprised.'

'I'm just amazed he didn't get found out before now if he was working that closely with children,' Wendy replied.

'Might well've done. All sorts of things get covered up. You see that with all these old telly stars for one.'

'True. What sort of material are we talking?'

'Mostly 8s and 9s, a couple of 5s and 6s,' Steve replied, referring to the COPINE scale for grading the severity of indecent images of children. The most severe level, 10, consisted of physical beating and whipping or involved an animal. 'That's not all, though. I ran his name through ViSOR. There's an expired RSHO.' A Risk of Sexual Harm Order was a record showing that an individual posed a serious risk to children because of at least two previous incidences of sexual contact or communication with a child under the age of sixteen. 'He'd been Facebook grooming, basically. He had the RSHO for two years, expired a few months back.'

'Christ. Makes Jeff Brelsford seem a bit flirty in comparison.'

'Well he was a dirty old bugger, but I see what you mean,' Steve said. 'Then again, so's Frank.'

The pair allowed themselves to chuckle for a moment. Sometimes you had to. The chuckling soon stopped, though, as soon as Malcolm Pope came swaggering into the room.

'What's the latest?' he demanded, without even saying hello.

Seeing an opportunity to cut a few words from her end-of-day report, Wendy decided to update him on the findings from Terry Kendall's laptop.

'I see,' Pope replied, typically non-committal. 'I must say, it makes you wonder how he managed to get away with it. You'd've thought he would've been caught by now. The team at Milton House are pretty hot on tracing people who download this sort of material.'

'Maybe not as hot as you thought,' Wendy said, unable to resist the dig.

'Indeed. No record on ViSOR, presumably?'

The incident room went very quiet as the other officers looked over at Debbie Weston, whose face was almost like a mannequin, or a rabbit caught in the headlights.

'You did run his details through ViSOR, didn't you, Detective Constable Weston?' Pope asked.

'Uh, I don't recall, sir,' Debbie replied. 'I've been doing a lot of paperwork. It's easy to get confused between—'

Pope held out his hand. 'Victim background checklist.'

Debbie lifted the pile of papers on her desk and began to sort through them until she found the sheet she was looking for. She handed it to Pope, who took a few seconds to scan down it, his face emotionless.

'You've ticked ViSOR lookup.'

'Oh. Well, I must have looked him up then.'

'Detective Sergeant Knight, will you run Terry Kendall's details through ViSOR?'

Wendy didn't much fancy being the one who landed a fellow officer in hot water. 'Sir, I'm not sure if we should—'

'Run Terry Kendall's details through ViSOR, Detective Sergeant Knight,' Pope repeated, his eyes never breaking contact with Debbie Weston's.

Wendy reluctantly did as she was told.

Her heart sank as she read the words on the screen in front of her.

'No charges, but listed as a potential risk to minors,' she whispered.

Malcolm Pope remained silent for a moment before blinking a few times and speaking in a quiet voice. 'The Chief Superintendent will be in touch soon, Detective Constable Weston.'

With that, he left the room.

## 27

As a police officer, interviewing people tended to be met with two distinct reactions. A good number of people would open up completely, feeling that they could trust the police and were able to tell them absolutely everything. On the other hand, there were many people who clammed up and didn't say a word about anything useful. The problem was that it wasn't always easy to work out which was happening. Quite often you'd think you were getting a lot of information from someone, only to find out it was either inaccurate or that they'd spoken a lot but said nothing.

When the impact of a person's crime ran deep, emotions tended to be much deeper too. It wasn't a simple case of anger, remorse, rage or forgiveness. What was on the surface was often there to mask something that was far more profound. They weren't straightforward feelings, either. It was entirely possible for a victim or relative to feel rage and forgiveness, either alternately or quite possibly at exactly the same time. The reactions to being a victim of a serious crime were wide-ranging and complex.

Wendy knew it was often best to try and get views from a range of people connected with a crime — their friends, family and colleagues — in order to really gain an understanding into how someone had been affected. Unfortunately, in most circumstances that just wasn't possible. Budget cuts and stretched time meant that it wasn't always feasible to gain as full an understanding as many officers would have liked.

In this particular case, though, it was vital that Wendy really understood what was going on in the minds of Katie McCourt's family and friends. After all, in this case some deep but hidden desire for revenge could have been the catalyst for murder.

She'd arranged to meet Suzanne Corrigan at the aptly-named Coffee House, nestled on the corner of the entrance and exit to one of the town's main car parks and barely a stone's throw from the back of Mildenheath Police Station. Almost opposite, one of the town's largest open spaces, the Recreation Ground, was home to a number of children braving the increasingly cold weather, blowing off some steam on the monkey bars and slides.

The Coffee House specialised in not only serving the usual tea and cakes, but also selling coffee, both ground and in full beans, to customers who wanted to make their own brews at home. Their main specialism, though, was flavoured 'gourmet' coffees, with varieties ranging from hazelnut and mint to brandy and cinnamon. Wendy was a fan of coffee, but she'd never yet found a flavoured version she liked, so had instead decided to opt for a cup of regular black filter.

She sat down at a vacant table and sipped at her mug. She was always uncomfortable being the first person to arrive anywhere, not quite knowing what to do with herself while she waited. She fished into her pocket for her mobile phone and had barely looked at it when Suzanne arrived and sat opposite her. A woman came over and took her order and Suzanne told her she'd have the same as Wendy.

'Can't stand that flavoured stuff,' she said, eliciting a smile from Wendy. 'Tastes like someone's splashed Britvic in it.'

After a few moments of dancing around the elephant in the room by chatting about irrelevant and inane topics, Wendy decided to bite the bullet.

'Suzanne, I wanted to talk to you a bit more about what happened to Katie.'

'I've told you more or less everything I know,' Suzanne said. 'It's the same as the account you had from her.'

'I know, but I wanted a bit more information on what happened after that,' Wendy explained.

Suzanne took a sip of her coffee and narrowed her eyes. 'What do you mean?'

'How it affected everyone, I mean. What effect it had on the family. I know from my job that something like that happening can have quite a deep impact on relatives. Parents in particular.'

'Well, yeah, John and Teresa were pretty cut up, obviously. You send your youngest daughter out to work for her first real job and she ends up getting felt up by some pervert. I don't think they were best pleased, if that's what you mean.'

Wendy sensed that Suzanne making light of the situation was probably something of a coping mechanism. She'd seen it a thousand times before.

'Deeper than that, though,' Wendy said. 'I can only imagine what it must be like for her parents. And for Anna.'

'It's a violation, isn't it?' Suzanne said. 'It's almost worse when it happens to your daughter or sister than it would be if it happened to you, if you see what I mean.'

'Is it still having an impact on them?' Wendy asked. 'They seemed pretty subdued when they were talking to me about it.'

Suzanne took another long sip of her coffee, seemingly thinking about how best to word her response.

'Between you and me, although they'd say it was something they'd dealt with and moved on from, I think John in particular is pretty cut up about it. I mean, I don't have any specific examples, but there's just the odd comments here and there. When you see the stuff on the TV or in the papers about child abuse, you know? The Jimmy Savile thing that came out, and now all the MPs and TV stars. Whenever that comes up in conversation or anything, it's like a dark cloud descends over him. But I suppose that's a subject that affects a lot of people. Everyone's got an opinion and it's the same one for a lot of people.'

'What sort of things does he say?' Wendy asked, her interest piqued.

'Oh, I can't remember specifics. The usual stuff, really. "String them up by their bollocks" and all that. He's not someone who's backwards in coming forwards, if you see what I mean. He's got some pretty tasty views on things like immigration and welfare, too, so I wouldn't say it surprised me when he comes out with that stuff.'

As she saw so often in her line of work, Wendy thought, a lack of understanding led to ignorance, which led to people having some pretty bizarre views.

'Can you remember anything specific that he said?' Wendy asked.

'No, I already told you. I've probably only met her parents a handful of times at family parties and things like that. When this all happened with Katie last year I tried to be there for them, be a good friend to Anna, so we spent a bit of time together then too. I didn't memorise the conversations, though.'

Wendy nodded. 'I understand. Would you say they've got better, though? In terms of moving on, I mean. Or is there still something lingering, perhaps growing?'

'Oh, it's definitely growing with John,' Suzanne said. 'They say it does with fathers, though. Katie had a new boyfriend about four months ago. He wanted to know absolutely everything about him. His name, his parents' names and jobs, where he lived, all that. Not just in a sense of being interested, I don't mean. He physically wouldn't let her see him again until she'd answered all his questions.'

Wendy tried not to let any emotions show on her face, and instead took a large gulp of coffee.

'Would you say he's overprotective, then?'

Suzanne pulled her lips back as she considered her response. 'In some ways, yes. I think mainly he's just overcautious, though. After all, he's seen what can happen.'

Wendy wasn't sure if that would be enough for her to justify spending time and resources on investigating John McCourt more closely, but it was certainly a starting point.

She steered the conversation towards more inert topics, talking about the scourge of traffic in the town and the lengths the council had gone to in order to finally secure a new bypass for Mildenheath — something which had been proposed for the best part of fifty years but had only just reached the construction phase.

In the meantime, shops and trade in the town had all but died, leaving the council with nothing but desperate measures.

Eventually, Suzanne managed to unavoidably bring the conversation back to Mildenheath CID and Jack Culverhouse in particular.

'So what's going on with him exactly? You seemed a bit cagey on the phone, but I guessed that was because you were at work.'

Wendy looked down at her coffee.

'Come on, Wendy. You said we were going to work together,' Suzanne said. 'I promise you I won't publish anything you don't want me to. I don't exactly want to be the kind of reporter who gloats over someone having a breakdown.'

'Breakdown?' Wendy asked, sensing an opportunity to turn the tables. 'Is that what you think's happened?'

'I don't know what to think,' Suzanne replied.

'Well why don't you give me your theories. Then I can tell you if you're right or wrong.' It was a classic police line, but it was one that tended to work more often than not.

Suzanne leant back in her chair and crossed her arms. 'Right, well my theory is that he was pretty close to PC Baxter. Saw himself as his mentor. Saw something of his younger self in him. Baxter took a bullet for him and died. That's got to really mess a man up, having that happen in front of his eyes.'

Wendy shook her head. 'That's not quite what happened.'

'It bloody was,' Suzanne said, her eyes widening. 'You seem to be forgetting I was there. It was my house.'

Wendy raised a hand to try and placate her. Suzanne had, thankfully, only been renting the house and had since moved, having not set foot in it since the night of Luke's death.

'I know, but what I mean is it's more complex than that. A big case like the Ripper one affects officers in more ways than one. He had to lead the case, he was responsible for it. And let's face it, five people died, including Luke.'

'So you admit that he's not well?' Suzanne asked.

Wendy looked her in the eye. 'Are we talking as friends or as police officer and reporter?'

'If you're asking whether or not you can trust me, I've already told you I won't print anything you don't want me to,' she replied.

'So why are you so keen to know? If you can't do anything with it, what does it matter?'

Suzanne sighed. 'I like Jack. He's a tough bugger, but he gets results. And I'm not going to lie, he makes for some bloody brilliant material in the paper. His quotes are unbeatable. Even from a purely selfish point of view, the last thing I want is some faceless bureaucrat taking his place and boring the pants off everybody.'

Wendy had to laugh. 'Well yes, he's certainly good

entertainment value, I'll give him that. Look, he's not been suspended or anything like that. Not officially, anyway, as far as I know. It's nothing disciplinary.' She knew she couldn't be sure of that herself — the updates from on high were few and far between — and she realised that perhaps she was just saying what she wanted to hear herself. 'He just needs time away from it all.'

'Has he been drinking?' Suzanne asked.

'It's Jack Culverhouse. He's never not been drinking.'

'You know what I mean. I don't just mean a couple of glasses of wine in the evening. I mean more heavily than that.'

Wendy leaned in towards Suzanne. 'Where are you getting this from?'

'Oh come on, Wendy. I saw him at Luke's memorial service. None of the other reporters did, but most of them have only seen short clips of him on the telly from the fall-out of the Ripper case. They don't know him personally. I recognised him straight away but thought it best not to say anything. He clearly wasn't his usual self, so I kept my distance.'

'You saw him?'

'Yeah, and he was a mess. Whatever you might think of me, Wendy, I'm not the sort of person who'd highlight something like that. I have some dignity.'

Wendy shook her head. 'I don't think badly of you, Suzanne, believe me. I've had to deal with a lot of reporters in my time and you're a long way from being anything like them. I just need to be cautious in how I deal with the press. It's a very sensitive subject.'

'I get that. But we're not talking as police officer and reporter, remember?'

Wendy held off for a second or two, considering her position, before smiling awkwardly.

## 28

That evening, Wendy decided to go to Culverhouse's place to see how he was getting on. She had to convince herself that she wasn't checking up on him, nor was she making sure he was still alive. Despite the way he'd acted recently, it wasn't particularly out of character for him and she felt a certain loyalty towards him — especially since Malcolm Pope had been on the scene.

It was the smell that hit her as Culverhouse opened his front door: the sweet, cloying smell of alcohol and the stuffiness of a house that hadn't seen an open window or door for days. She could see he hadn't shaved, either. There was a good few days' growth starting to show and she thought it actually looked quite good on him, aside from the fact that it had only come about through laziness and neglect.

She tried not to visit Culverhouse at home if she could

help it. The way it was looking and smelling right now, she didn't particularly want to come back again any time soon. Culverhouse was a private man who kept himself to himself. He was the sort of person everyone thought they knew quite well, but that was because he always had something to say and had always been a larger-than-life character. But when they thought about it, they realised that he'd never actually told them anything about himself.

He'd opened up to Wendy once, but only once and not as much as she would've liked. She guessed everyone needed a release every now and again, particularly in this job. That was why so many police officers' marriages fell apart. It was the sort of job where you needed to talk about it in order to stop yourself going mad, but the nature of the job meant you weren't able to.

'How have you been?' she asked as he removed a grease-smeared plate from the arm of the sofa and beckoned for her to sit down.

'How do I look?'

'Like shit,' she replied.

'Charming. I'll have you know I had takeaway pizza off this plate. It came in a box and I plated it up, so I've not lost all my dignity. Granted, that was three days ago, but still.'

At any other time, Wendy would've laughed at his self-deprecating wit, but she knew by now that it was just a defence mechanism.

'What's new?' he asked, calling from the kitchen as he

tidied the plate away. 'Malcolm Pope got you licking his arse yet?'

'I don't think we're far off,' Wendy replied. 'Let's just say it's... different with him around.'

'Careful. Next thing you know, you'll be telling me you miss me.'

Wendy didn't respond to that. 'Steve and Frank aren't happy. Debbie's not bothered, though.'

'She never is. You could put Pol Pot in charge and she'd just sit in the corner getting on with her paperwork. She's dependable. Reliable. Not likely to be distracted by someone opening a pub door four miles away.'

Wendy chuckled. 'Steve's been cutting down, actually. Probably something to do with having to spend an extra hour or two writing up bloody reports for Pope. Doubt if he even makes last orders any more.'

Culverhouse returned from the kitchen and sat down in an armchair. 'He won't put up with that for long. He'll go stir crazy. He's the sort of bloke who needs to have his set ways.'

'Tell me about it,' Wendy replied. 'Sometimes I think he and Frank are on the verge of breaking into some sort of revolution. They're talking about going to the Chief Constable to complain.'

Culverhouse shook his head. 'Won't do any good. They're between a rock and a hard place. If they go straight to the top they'll be seen as troublemakers. Chain of command dictates they have to go to the Superintendent or Chief Superintendent. Problem with that is the Chief Super's got the whole of the merged county forces to look after and the Super's too busy creaming over Malcolm Pope to care.'

He was right. The most senior Detective Superintendent was one of Pope's biggest fans, and it was highly suspected that Pope would follow him up the ladder once the Chief Constable retired. The Chief Superintendent might have been more sympathetic towards them but they never saw hide nor hair of her, especially as she had to spread herself across three collaborative county forces.

The structure within and around Mildenheath CID was an odd one, not helped by the fact that it had been effectively isolated as an almost self-sufficient satellite department. With Chief Constable Charles Hawes choosing to base himself largely at Mildenheath, the CID team at the station had a direct route to the top. The fact that he was very sympathetic towards them helped enormously. To all intents and purposes, the fact that there was a Superintendent and Chief Superintendent between them in the hierarchy didn't matter a bit. They were all too busy shuffling paper up at Milton House, waiting for Mildenheath to fail and be swallowed up into the wider organisation.

'Suzanne Corrigan's been sniffing around,' Wendy said, getting straight to the point.

'Tell her to bugger off then.'

'She's not stupid,' Wendy replied. 'She's already been asking about links between the two killings. And she knows about Jeff Brelsford's history, too.'

'How?' Culverhouse asked, his eyebrows narrowing.

'Some family connection. I put some pressure on her and persuaded her not to run with anything. I think we can trust her, but that's not the point.'

Culverhouse looked at her silently for a few seconds. 'What did you mean about links?'

Bollocks. She hadn't meant to say that. She made a non-committal 'Hmmmm?' and looked towards the window.

'You said she's been asking about links between the two killings. What links?'

Wendy sighed. 'I really shouldn't be telling you this. The guy killed in Southbrook. Terry Kendall. He had a hard drive full of child porn. He and Jeff Brelsford were killed in the same way, too. Almost certainly by the same person.'

Culverhouse looked at her and said nothing for a moment. 'Good,' he finally said.

'Good?'

'Yeah, good. At least someone's getting rid of the buggers. You can't stop someone being a paedophile, Knight. They don't get rehabilitated like burglars. It's a disease of the mind. One that can't be cured.'

'You don't know that,' Wendy replied.

Culverhouse snorted. 'How many reformed paedophiles have you heard of? It doesn't happen. You're in Cloud Cuckoo Land again. Besides which, do you know how many of them get off and get away with it? They're a menace to society. If someone's doing our job for us, I really couldn't give a shit.'

'Are you serious?' Wendy asked, knowing full well that he was deadly serious but hoping that he wasn't.

'Listen, Knight,' he replied, looking her in the eye. 'Sometimes you just have to accept that the world isn't perfect. We can't save the day every time.'

Wendy shook her head in disbelief. 'So what do you suggest we do? Just sit back and let him get on with it? Give him the medal of honour for helping us out?'

'Policing's changed in my time,' Culverhouse said, seeming to ignore the question. 'They bang on about all this collaborative shit now, but that's bollocks. It's not collaborative. Back when I started, the focus was on getting the murderers, rapists and criminals off the streets. Whatever it took. If someone else was doing our job for us, we let them get on with it. That's fucking collaborative.'

'There's no excuse!' Wendy replied, now starting to get severely worried about him. 'What if this person thinks they've identified another person who's a paedophile or whatever and they're wrong? He's already playing fast and loose with his definition by killing Jeff Brelsford. Who's to say he's going to get the right person every time?'

Culverhouse shrugged his shoulders. 'Policing's always carried risks. Always will.'

'But this is more than a risk. We're talking about innocent people potentially being harmed or killed.'

'And for what reason?' Culverhouse replied quickly, the words practically tripping over themselves. 'I'll tell you what reason. Because those bastards are harming innocent people anyway. Innocent children. We're talking about paedophiles here, not fucking Greenpeace activists.'

'I knew I shouldn't have told you,' Wendy said quietly, almost whispered. 'In fact, I shouldn't have come here. I can't help you. You can't even help yourself.'

Culverhouse said nothing and sat with his chin propped on his hand, staring at the wall. After a few seconds, Wendy got up and left.

Driving home, she started to become more and more infuriated with Culverhouse. Who did he think he was, trying to justify gangs of vigilantes taking the law into their own hands? He'd always been a dinosaur with some pretty backward ideas, but this was something else. He was almost defending what they were doing. He'd seemed offended that Wendy didn't agree with him and support it too. That struck her as being particularly odd.

Jack Culverhouse had changed recently, there was no

doubt about that. He'd become far more unstable and she'd found it increasingly difficult to predict his actions.

She had to think of something else. She ran through the facts of the case to distract herself. Both murder victims had a history of sexual contact with young people and had been listed on ViSOR as sexual offenders. The vigilante theory was looking strong. That's when it hit her. Jack Culverhouse would've had access to ViSOR.

## 29

Like most officers at Mildenheath, Wendy tried to avoid going to Milton House wherever possible. This time, though, she knew she had no choice. She'd timed her visit carefully, but had still sat waiting in the canteen for almost half an hour before she saw Xavier Moreno come in for his lunch. That was the best thing about the techies and lab geeks: they could always rely on actually having a lunch break and having it at around the same time each day.

Xavier was instantly recognisable, even though Wendy had only met him once or twice. His olive skin and striking Hispanic looks had come from his father — as had his name — even though he'd never set foot in Spain in his life.

Wendy didn't need to go over and initiate a conversation; she knew he'd be over like a shot as soon as he saw her. For someone who worked for the police, he hadn't been particularly good at hiding his attraction to Wendy the last time they'd met.

'Wendy!' she heard him call as he came over to her table with a packaged sandwich and a mug of coffee. 'What are you doing here?'

Wendy smiled. 'Got to pop by every now and then, unfortunately. Show them I'm still alive.'

'It's good to see you,' Xavier said, smiling back. 'How are things down at Mildenheath?'

'Yeah, good. Keeping busy as always,' Wendy replied.

'So I hear. Still, at least you've taken Malcolm Pope off our hands, so I suppose we'd better thank you for that,' he said, laughing.

Wendy laughed too. 'Christ, doesn't anyone like him?'

'The big cheeses. All except the Chief Constable, that is, but he won't be around forever. Everyone above him loves him, but anyone who actually has to deal with his shit can't stand him. He wants everything yesterday. I've never seen anyone fuck up a computer as often as he does. Do you know how many new logins we have to do for him? He's a nightmare.'

Wendy laughed again, mostly to ingratiate Xavier. 'Funny thing is, he'd be the first one to make someone feel like shit for forgetting their logins.'

'Exactly! What a dick, man.'

It was things like that which showed Wendy that Xavier was perhaps a little too young in the mind for her.

'Listen, Xav. I was wondering if you might be able to do me a favour. Off the record, I mean.'

Xavier sucked air in through his teeth in mock disgust. 'Off the record? Blimey, they're not words we tend to hear all that often around here with DCI Pope about.'

'Yeah, well he's wormed his way into my office for the foreseeable future so you're clear.'

'What is this exactly?' Xavier asked. 'I know we're good friends and that, but I'm not going to put my job on the line.'

'No, no, nothing like that,' Wendy said, smiling to placate him. 'I just need to know about some computer records. You know Jack Culverhouse has been put on leave? Well, I need to look into something,' she lied. 'But you can't say anything to anyone. This is strictly on the QT.'

'What is it?' he asked.

'I need a log of Culverhouse's ViSOR searches. Dates, times, records he looked at.'

Xavier rubbed his mouth and scratched his head. 'Christ, Wendy. I dunno. Investigating a serving officer? That's more than my job's worth. You'd have to go through the Chief Constable for that.'

'I have,' Wendy lied. 'By which I mean he asked me to speak to you. He has his suspicions but says it needs to be handled carefully. Again, this is all strictly between the two of us.'

'Bloody hell. I thought Hawes was good mates with Culverhouse?'

Wendy nodded. 'They get on. That's why this needs to be kept quiet.'

'Right, I see. Well, I mean, it's possible to do. I'm the system admin for our force. There's no-one above me, practically speaking, who'd be able to see that I'd looked. The Chief Constable could technically request the records from the central server admins to see what I'd been up to, but if this is all at his request...'

'Exactly. He'd have to go through the IPCC or take it central. That'd leave a paper trail, which he doesn't want in case he's wrong.'

Xavier sighed. 'I'll think on it, alright? I'm not saying I won't — I want to help you, really I do — I just need to think it over and make sure we're watertight on this. It's possible, but I don't want to take any unnecessary risks.'

Wendy smiled, leant over and kissed Xavier on the cheek. 'Thanks, Xav. You're an absolute star.'

That should be enough to tip him over the edge and onto her side, she thought.

## 30

He was in a quandary. He'd majorly fucked up with Terry
Kendall and he knew it. If that bloody woman hadn't come
nosing round he could've tied up all the loose ends just
how he wanted, but he'd been made to change his plans at
the last minute. He didn't like that one bit.

He should've been onto the next target by now, but
something was stopping him. He worried it might be fear,
but told himself it was just caution. Being fearful right now
just wouldn't do. No, it was caution. He'd come close to
being spotted — might even have been spotted — and he
couldn't risk it again so soon.

The plan had to be adhered to, though. After all, no-
one else was going to give these bastards what they
deserved. These prats masquerading as police officers and
detectives certainly weren't going to dish out justice. Not

justice as he saw it, anyway. As far as he was concerned, real justice died a long time ago.

Thankfully, he had two prongs of attack. Two ways of sourcing his targets. He'd used one as a backup for the other up until now, but he had started to consider that it might be wise to drop one. After all, if the police somehow managed to start following a trail, there was always a likelihood that he could be discovered. Nothing was ever completely untraceable — he'd found that much out a long time ago and up until now had used it to his advantage.

No, he was going to have to alter his plans slightly. He knew the police would possibly be expecting him to do so, and in many ways that's what they were counting on: getting him out of his comfort zone and hoping he made a mistake which would lead them to him without them having to actually do the legwork. That was how things worked.

What they wouldn't expect, though, would be that he'd move onto a backup plan, just as well rehearsed as his main plan. They probably wouldn't even be able to tie up the links. That was the gamble he was going to have to take, anyway. It'd need a new mindset, a new psychological approach, but that was fine with him.

He popped another square of chocolate into his mouth. He'd almost gone through the whole bar in the last ten minutes, but he didn't care. Life had always been good to him in that way. He'd never put on weight, never lost his hair and never had many of the worries that other people had in everyday life. His worries went much deeper. He was worried for society, for humanity as a whole. And he was going to fix it.

## 31

Fortunately for Wendy, Xavier Moreno had had the good sense to phone her on her private mobile. She knew she'd taken a different kind of risk in giving him that number, but she supposed it wouldn't do her any harm to string him along for a bit. After all, he could prove to be very useful.

She tried not to sound too desperate as she answered the phone, keeping her excitement in check. She knew that whatever Xavier told her would steer the investigation off in one sharp direction or another.

She hoped her suspicions weren't correct. Not only would that potentially mean that everything she'd believed about Jack Culverhouse had been wrong, but from a purely selfish point of view it would be impossible to ever look Malcolm Pope in the eye again. Not only would Culverhouse be ruined, but Pope would be the golden boy for evermore.

'Hi Xavier,' she said, as calmly as she could.

'Hi. I've got some news on the logs you asked me to look at,' Xavier said. 'Now, I've got to point out that someone looking at ViSOR records doesn't really mean much in itself. I mean, it's not looked at all that commonly by DCIs unless they're specifically investigating a sex-related case, but it's not rare enough to be immediately suspicious, if you see what I mean.'

'Yes, I understand,' Wendy said, hoping he'd get to the point.

'The only way you'd be able to really say if something was a little bit odd was if records were being looked up when they had nothing to do with an active case that the officer was assigned to. That tends to be a bit of a red herring, but doesn't necessarily mean anything. Now, first things first, Culverhouse hasn't looked at anyone's specific records in a few months, and he's never specifically looked up the names of either Jeff Brelsford or Terry Kendall. But that's not all.'

'Just tell me,' Wendy said, annoyed at Xavier's dramatic pause.

'He did do a radius search on all known offenders living within a ten mile radius, three days before Jeff Brelsford was killed. Brelsford would've shown up on the search.'

'But you said he didn't look up their names, right?' Wendy asked.

'Yes, true. But that doesn't necessarily mean anything. If he'd looked up their names and viewed records, that would've left a trace. He would've known that, too, so wouldn't have wanted to risk it. Let's just say, for argument's sake, that he does the radius search. The names pop up. He can't risk going into any records and leaving a trace, so he jots some names down on paper. He could find their details out in any way he liked. Electoral roll? Phone book? He's a detective, Wendy. He could find a way.'

'Jesus,' Wendy said, trying to take it all in. 'So what's your instinct?'

Xavier laughed. 'I don't do instincts. I leave that to your lot. I do databases. And that's what the database says.'

Wendy realised she had a lot of thinking to do. Having been working on Culverhouse's team for a while now, she knew that he had no reason to be looking up sexual offenders on ViSOR. They hadn't dealt with a sexual crime for some time — that tended to go straight to Milton House — and the period leading up to Jeff Brelsford's killing had been particularly slow, with the team working on the tail end of some organised crime and fraud cases. Certainly nothing that would have meant Jack Culverhouse needing to search ViSOR.

'Is there nothing more?' Wendy asked, desperate to know either way what this meant. Her mind was becoming so clouded with confusion that she just wanted Xavier to tell her definitively either way if Culverhouse was involved. The rational part of her brain knew that he couldn't possibly make that judgement call, but right now she wasn't sure she was capable of it either.

'Not that I can see,' Xavier said. 'But like I said, it doesn't mean too much on its own. It could be entirely innocent.'

'But it might not be,' Wendy said before her brain could stop her.

Xavier paused before speaking. 'That's for you to decide, Wendy.'

She thought back to what she already knew. Marius, Jeff Brelsford's neighbour from across the road, had seen a man with dark hair wearing a suit heading up Jeff Brelsford's front path on the night he was murdered. Yes, the description fitted Culverhouse, but it could also fit practically any other person. It was extremely unlikely, she thought, that a Detective Chief Inspector — and especially one who'd been in the national news recently — would just brazenly walk up a garden path in the middle of Mildenheath and kill a man at his front door. Then again, she knew damn well that Jack Culverhouse had been remarkably unpredictable recently. What was to say he hadn't just gone completely off the rails?

No. She was being stupid, she told herself. How could she even suspect him? She'd put two and two together and come up with a thousand. It was all circumstantial at best, but it still didn't stop the nagging doubt at the back of her brain. After all, in the frame of mind Jack Culverhouse had been in recently, absolutely anything was possible.

## 32

One of the first things Wendy had realised after joining the police force was that you should never be surprised by anything. Just when you thought you'd seen it all, something else would pop up when you least expected it and throw a huge spanner in the works.

The realisation had stunned her. That Jack Culverhouse could not only have been reluctant to investigate a murder was shocking enough, but not entirely surprising. The possibility that he could have been more directly involved, though, was something else.

Her instinct was that she needed to speak to someone about this, but she was severely limited in her options. Frank, Debbie and Steve were completely out of the question as their loyalty to Culverhouse was stronger than hers. Going to Malcolm Pope or Charles Hawes would be equally stupid, as it would to speak to just about any serving officer. It struck her again that she had very, very few people she knew from outside the police force.

There was only one person she could speak to. Someone who knew the pressures of the job. Someone who knew Jack Culverhouse at his rawest and what he was capable of.

She'd not even properly thought about how to attack the subject as she found herself walking up Robin Grundy's driveway and ringing his doorbell. He answered the door a few seconds later, smiling happily. Wendy supposed that he never smiled quite that readily when he was a serving police officer. That would have been something that had come with retirement.

She decided that this time she would accept Robin's offer of a cup of tea. After all, it seemed as though this could be quite a long and drawn-out chat. She knew she couldn't give too much away — this was a situation in which she knew she couldn't trust anyone — and she needed to be very careful indeed as to how she tried to elicit information from Grundy. After all, he was a far more seasoned detective than she was.

'Did you go to see Jack?' he asked, before taking a sip of his steaming mug of tea.

'We've spoken,' Wendy replied. 'I'm still trying to figure out how to win him round. I wanted to talk to you about something completely different, though.'

'Sounds interesting. Go on,' Robin said, taking another sip of tea.

Wendy sighed. 'I don't know how much I can tell you. The thing is, there's been some suspicion that one or two officers might be involved in some shady dealings.' That should be vague enough, she thought.

'What kind of shady dealings?' Robin asked.

'I can't really say. Sorry. But it involves feeding information to people who shouldn't have it.'

Robin nodded. 'This to do with the Ripper case?'

Wendy saw no reason to dissuade him of that assumption. 'Yes. Yes, it is.'

'Thought so,' Robin said. 'I did wonder how the press had so much information at the time. There's no way I would've passed that level of detail onto them and I doubted very much if Jack Culverhouse would've done. It's always been a big problem, though. Not as much as it used to be, mind. In my day there were more officers passing information onto the criminals than the press.'

She decided not to tell Grundy that her suspicions were exactly that. It'd have no bearing on what she asked next.

'I was thinking of perhaps asking for Jack's help,' she lied. 'But I'm not sure if I can. What would you suggest I do?'

'His help in what?' Grundy asked, cocking his head.

Wendy sighed. 'I really don't know. Look, I shouldn't

even be here. I just feel... I dunno. I can't really speak to anyone at the station about things as they're too close to the whole situation. Plus everyone's being careful about what they say with Malcolm Pope about. The whole atmosphere's toxic. And with Jack the way he is, he's hardly the best listening ear in the world.'

'Is he ever?' Grundy said, chuckling.

Wendy chuckled too. 'True. I guess sometimes I just need to speak to someone who understands but isn't directly in the situation, do you know what I mean?'

'I know exactly what you mean,' Grundy said, smiling. 'I suppose that's one of the good things about the way things have changed. If something affects you at work these days you've got counsellors on hand and all sorts.'

'Yeah, at Milton House,' Wendy said. 'Hardly the best place to go when you're feeling depressed or despondent. It's enough to finish you off.'

Grundy looked at her for a few moments. 'So what's this really all about?'

'How do you mean?' Wendy asked.

'Well, you haven't just come here for a social chat in the middle of a murder investigation, have you?'

Wendy looked at the floor. 'Not exactly, no.'

'So why don't you tell me?'

Wendy swallowed. 'Jack's worrying me. I can't go into the details, but there's only really a limited number of people who could be involved with these killings. He's been acting very suspiciously and some things just don't seem right.'

'You think he's involved?' Grundy asked.

Wendy forced a smile. 'Do you think it's possible?'

'Well, that's a big thing to ask. Personally? No. Jack wouldn't get involved with anything like that. He's determined, sure. A stubborn old bugger. But above all else, he's principled. He sticks to his beliefs.'

'That's what I'm worried about,' Wendy replied.

'How do you mean?'

'I mean I'm not just worried about him being *involved* somehow. I'm worried that he might be the murderer.'

The reassuring expression on Grundy's face slowly dropped. 'I think perhaps we ought to have a drink.'

## 33

Wendy needed answers. Whether Jack Culverhouse was involved or not, it didn't actually matter. The problem was she needed to know either way. The thought that her trust could have been broken in that way was devastating, but the possibility that she could have thought such a thing about Jack if it was untrue would potentially be even worse. Whatever the truth was, she needed it.

Her distinct lack of self esteem meant that she was certain there was no way she could outwit Jack. He'd always be one step ahead, so trying to prove anything would be futile. She was sure that she knew him pretty well by now, though. A lot of the time, she could see through him. His macho attitude and bravado was just one big cover — she'd learnt that much fairly early on — and she reckoned she knew what buttons to press. She saw that it was to her advantage to strike while he was clearly not as stable as he had been, and took the opportunity.

Jack didn't seem the slightest bit surprised to see her when he opened his front door, but he didn't immediately stand aside to let her in.

'What?' he said, his eyes glazed.

'Can I come in?' Wendy asked, tilting her head.

'Are you sure you want to? It's probably not up to your standards.'

Wendy closed her eyes. 'Don't be daft. I'm here to speak to you, not to inspect your cleaning.'

Culverhouse shrugged and stepped aside. Wendy could smell the alcohol fumes as she walked past him, the stale fug of the house hitting her in the face like a sledge-hammer as she made her way through to the conservatory at the back, assuming that this would be the least unpleasant room to sit in.

She sat down on a wicker chair as Culverhouse hovered around in the doorway. 'Do you want a drink?' he asked.

'No, thanks,' Wendy replied. 'Guv, can you sit down please? I need to speak to you about something.'

He looked at her for a couple of seconds, then did as he was told.

'First things first, I don't want you to go off the head at me, okay? I just want to speak calmly and rationally so I can move on with this investigation.'

He looked at her for another couple of seconds. 'What the fuck are you talking about?'

Wendy breathed out heavily. 'When you said you wanted to shake the hand of whoever had killed Jeff Brelsford, did you mean it?'

Culverhouse's tone was neutral but firm. 'If you're asking me whether I'd rather spend the evening with a live Jeff Brelsford or the man who killed him, I'd take the latter every time.'

Wendy swallowed. 'And if you knew who was doing it, or had suspicions as to who it was, would you withhold that information or make it known?'

His face didn't change. 'What's that supposed to mean?'

She didn't quite know how to phrase it. 'Look, we've had some information come to light. This isn't easy for me to say.'

'For fuck's sake, Knight, will you spit it out?' His voice rose in volume.

Wendy looked him straight in the eye. 'Why did you look up a list of offenders on ViSOR three days before Jeff Brelsford was killed?'

She thought she saw a flicker of something move across his face.

'I'm a DCI,' he said impassively. 'It's my job to look at lists of offenders.'

'Not sex offenders. Not at that point. You weren't

working on any cases involving sex offenders,' Wendy replied, leaning in closely. She heard his breathing becoming louder and thought she saw his jaw clench.

'It was to do with another case,' he said, finally.

'Guv, tell me the truth. I deserve that much.' Wendy could feel herself close to tears. 'Who's next, Jack?'

'Are you having a fucking laugh?' he barked. 'Why are you always so blinkered? Do you seriously think I'm going around popping off paedos?'

Wendy closed her eyes. 'I don't know what to think any more.'

'Right. Great. Thanks very much. As if things couldn't get any better.'

'Just tell me,' Wendy said, her voice breaking.

'I'll tell you one thing and one thing only,' he said, standing up. 'I'll tell you that if after all we've been through together, as a team, that you think I'm some sort of turn-coat, then you can forget it. You can fucking forget it!' he yelled, swiping his arm across the side unit, a pile of papers and glass ornaments crashing to the conservatory floor as Wendy watched.

'Now,' he said, his voice much calmer. 'You've got two options. Do you trust me or are you going to throw away everything we've worked for over the years?'

## 34

Frank Vine found Wendy in a rather less positive mood than usual that morning. He was pretty sure, though, that the information he'd had from Bower and Sons' web hosting company would brighten her day a bit.

'Right,' he said, plonking his notebook down on the desk and explaining its contents to spare Wendy the trouble of having to try and decipher his handwriting. 'I managed to do all this without calling the tech team, which I'm pretty bloody pleased about.'

'All what?' Wendy asked.

'Finding out who'd nabbed the registration number for the Vauxhall Combo off the website of the van hire company in Birmingham. They've got a .co.uk domain name, right? So I went to Nominet. That's the domain registry. Their records showed the website is hosted by a company called Edge Online. I got onto this Edge company and sent over a formal request for the server logs. Took a bit of time, unfortunately, but they came back to me and even helped to interpret the information. I couldn't make head nor tail of it. Turns out the IP addresses — the identifier of the internet connections used to connect to the website — were mostly from the Birmingham area, funnily enough. Their website doesn't get many hits at all, apparently. A couple from the States, India and the Philippines, which was a bit weird but pretty normal according to the bloke at Edge. What was really interesting was a visit two months back from an IP address in the Mildenheath area.'

Wendy cocked her head and looked at him. 'Jesus, Frank. How did you manage that? You're still struggling with light switches.'

Frank grinned from ear to ear. 'I know, right? Who needs these computer forensics blokes anyway?'

'So do we have an ID on a suspect?' Wendy asked.

'Not quite. The IP address only tells us which exchange the connection was made from. Can be hundreds of physical properties using that exchange, if not thousands.'

'Great,' Wendy said. 'So all we know is that it's someone in the Mildenheath area? We'd guessed that much already.'

'Not quite,' Frank said. 'With that IP address we're able to go to the internet service provider and get something more specific. Much more specific. Like a name and address.'

'And why haven't you?'

'I have,' Frank said. 'And that's where it gets really interesting.'

'Jesus Christ, Frank! Just get to the point, will you?' Wendy said, her voice rising in both pitch and volume.

'Right, sorry,' Frank said, shuffling his feet. 'They traced it to an address in Ambassador Court. A customer called Kyle Finney. I've looked on the PNC and the really interesting thing is he's got form himself. Listed on ViSOR, as it happens. Released from Her Maj's pleasure six months ago after touching up schoolgirls in the park. The guv had been trying to nab him for ages, apparently, so he's known. DCI Pope's given us clearance to go and speak to him.'

'Speak to him?' Wendy said, standing up and grabbing her coat. 'We're going to have him.'

Frank Vine stood and smiled. 'Y'know, Wendy, you're starting to behave more like the guv every day.'

Wendy shot Frank a look of humoured displeasure. 'Fuck off, Frank.'

## 35

Jack Culverhouse was glad he was the sort of person who didn't give a shit what people thought of him. As if the looks and double-takes from his former colleagues on spotting him walking around the station in week-old clothes, unshaved and with unkempt hair weren't enough, the ignominy of having to be buzzed through doors that only a few weeks ago he could open himself was truly humiliating. This was his lair, his domain. And now he was a stranger in his own world, unable to even open a door for himself. That was the ultimate insult.

By the time he got up to Charles Hawes's office, he was ready to rumble. Hawes ushered him in and Culverhouse sat down on the plush chair.

'I'm going to get straight to the point, Jack,' Hawes said. 'There's a reason I asked you to come here. I'm retiring.'

Culverhouse said nothing for a moment. 'What the fuck? No you're not.'

Hawes smiled. 'I'm not getting any younger, Jack. I have to retire at some point.'

'Why now?'

'Look, things have changed recently. The force isn't the same as it was before. You know that as well as anybody.'

'Yeah, and that's exactly why we have to stay exactly where we are and fight back against the bastards. If you go now, this place won't be standing in a year's time. You know that.'

'Yes, Jack. I know that,' the Chief Constable said. 'But I can't keep working until I'm a hundred and five just to keep a pile of bricks and mortar standing. Change is inevitable. Sure, we can postpone it but we can't stop it. And I know one thing sure as hell: Malcolm Pope will be here long after I'm gone. He's young. He's got time on his side. All he has to do is wait for me to go.'

'So you're just going to let him?' Culverhouse shouted, incredulous.

'I don't have much choice. I can't stop getting older. I'm always going to have the best part of twenty years on him. There's nothing I can do about nature. I might as well go now while I've at least got one shred of dignity and before this place completely crushes me.'

'That's bullshit and you know it,' Culverhouse barked.

'It's no use, Jack. My mind's made up. I'll be sending a statement to the papers later today. But I thought it was best that you knew first. I had to tell you in person.'

Culverhouse crossed his arms and sat back. 'Why me? I'm not even a police officer at the moment. If you think back carefully, you'll remember that you had me suspended.'

'You're on leave, Jack. There's a difference.'

'There's no fucking difference at all,' he replied. 'It's just more bullshit wording to try and make things sound better. Right from the school of Malcolm bloody Pope.'

'Listen, Jack. The reason I'm telling you is because there's something I need to say. We've been fighting back against the tide of change for years, and it's a fucking tsunami now. It's pointless resisting. I'm getting out while I still can and taking the pension. You've put years and years into this service and this police force. The last thing I want is for you to carry on as you are, get kicked out and lose the lot.'

'So what are you saying?' Culverhouse asked, cocking his head.

'I'm saying you need to mellow out a bit. A lot. Roll with the punches. Give yourself a chance of at least seeing out the rest of your service with a new Chief Constable. Because we both know you won't last five minutes if you carry on as you have been.'

Culverhouse stared at Hawes. 'Jesus Christ. You've

fallen for it too, haven't you? Malcolm Pope's bullshit. He's turned you as well.'

Hawes shook his head violently and raised a hand. 'No, Jack, no-one's turned me. This isn't some batshit conspiracy theory. It's a case of recognising when we've been fighting a battle for far longer than we've needed to and accepting that we're in the minority — a minority which is dwindling. Hell, if I wasn't Chief Constable there's no way either of us would still be serving officers.'

'But it's not just a case of that, is it?' Culverhouse said, his voice raised. 'What about Steve and Frank? I can't see them becoming pen pushers. You can't just up and leave because the pressure's getting too much. That's what we have Chief Constables for.'

Hawes stood up and walked to the drinks cabinet, pouring himself a glass of water from the jug, which sat on top of it. 'With all due respect, Jack, it's not your decision to make.'

'So what's next? Who takes your job?'

'Who knows? Not up to me. Usual protocol is to ask the outgoing Chief Constable for their recommendation, but they don't have to. Almost certainly won't ask me, and if they do they'll do the opposite of what I say. Choice is down to Martin Cummings at the end of the day.'

Hearing things like this always enraged Culverhouse. The elected Police and Crime Commissioner was nothing more than a politician sucking wages and resources from the police force whilst using it to further his own political agenda. His main focus was on reducing what he called 'wastage', which, funnily enough, didn't stretch to his own salary and ludicrous expenses, but instead consisted of frontline police officers, desk staff and community policing resources.

'Bastard. He'd do away with a Chief Constable if he could,' Culverhouse said. 'He'd have a Community Enforcement Manager or some bollocks like that.'

Hawes laughed. 'I don't think so. But the new Chief would very likely be someone who sympathises with his aims and objectives. That means Mildenheath will almost certainly be merged into Milton House.'

'Well there's only one option, then, isn't there?' Culverhouse said. 'You're going to have to stay.'

Hawes shook his head. 'Not going to happen, Jack. My mind's made up.'

'So's mine,' Culverhouse said, standing and pushing his chair in. 'If you're going to make a stupid decision that brings this department crashing down and gives Malcolm Pope carte blanche to do whatever the fuck he wants, you're doing it without my blessing. Enjoy your retirement.'

With that, he walked out.

36

This was a familiar pattern for Jack Culverhouse. Just when he thought life couldn't fuck him over any more, it went and found a way. Work had been his only constant in life. Everything else had chopped and changed and provided him with far too much drama, but work had always been there. Sure, it was far from being a consistent job in terms of what he'd have to deal with every day, but at least he knew where he stood.

In his personal life, things were far from secure. Ever since Helen had upped and left, citing his obsession with work as her reason, he'd become even more driven by the job. After all, it was the only thing he could rely on. Now, though, even that had been taken from him. If it had been purely his own stupid fault, he could at least come to terms with that eventually. But the fact that this seemed to be one massive fit-up with Malcolm Pope at the centre made the whole situation even more bitter.

Pope had been trying to get rid of him for a long time, he knew that. But while the two men were contemporaries there was nothing he could do. With Hawes retiring, he knew exactly what would happen. They'd promote from within, the cretins at Milton House would all shuffle up a rung, Mildenheath would be closed and merged into the main CID unit and he'd find himself increasingly ostracised. There might even be redundancies.

His head was telling him he was getting too old for this shit. Hawes was right. The best thing for both of them would be to put it all behind them and either move forward and adapt or get out and take the pension. Jack Culverhouse wasn't a man who was often driven by his head, though. He was a man who followed his heart, and his heart was telling him to stick two fingers up to the bastards and carry on as he'd always been — the way that had always got results. After all, he'd solved far more serious crimes than Malcolm Pope.

The trouble was, his record counted for nothing. Orders from on high were orders from on high, and he knew plenty of excellent police officers who'd been shuffled off to the retirement home over his years. He was old school, and he knew that wasn't popular. He knew that people equated that with roughing up villains, planting evidence and taking bungs.

To him, though, it meant being able to do the job in a way which actually put his skills to some use. It meant following his detective's nose. It meant ensuring that you got the right person, no matter what, and without allowing them to wriggle free on a technicality or to slip out the back door while you waited for some piece of paperwork to be signed off by a manager.

No, he had to fight it. But without the backing of a Chief Constable who came from the same background and was sympathetic to his opinions, how far could he get? Not very far, he guessed. With Charles Hawes gone, he'd be a lone wolf with no backing from anyone above him in the food chain. He'd be increasingly ostracised, left to fend for himself under the pressure of having to conform or else. And they had the right to refer to the old-school officers as corrupt bullies. It was always the same — the new order comes in under a banner of reform and just replaces it with the same old shit under a different colour or name.

Jack's problem was that he was a proud man. He knew that could often be his downfall. Retirement just wasn't an option for him. He knew he had to fight and stand up for what he believed in and he knew that probably wouldn't do him any favours, but he was a man of principle. He'd rather die fighting than wave the white flag and take the money.

What worried him most was the nagging doubts that crawled into his mind. He never used to have those. He always used to plough on regardless, not even thinking of an alternative to his way of doing things. There was no such word as futile. It was always worth fighting for what he believed in. Now, though, he realised he was getting old, starting to wonder whether or not it was worth the effort. The thought of an early retirement, a cash payout and retiring somewhere sunny certainly appealed.

He didn't need the money. Not really. When Helen had disappeared, she'd effectively relinquished her right to half of the house, as far as he was concerned. He'd considered having her declared dead and taking on sole ownership himself, but had decided against it. Now she'd reappeared, that whole seven-year process would have to begin again. He'd also have to show that he'd gone to extraordinary lengths to find her, which he just wasn't prepared to do. Besides, he knew Helen wasn't dead. Still, half of the house would see him more than alright in retirement.

He'd been earning a decent sum of money for a good few years now, and had very limited outgoings. Fifty-five grand a year went a long way when you lived by yourself and did nothing other than work. He never really knew how much money he had in the bank at any given time. He knew it was enough to not bother himself worrying about as it'd been increasing month-on-month ever since he could remember.

He supposed that with a nice payoff and pension he

could easily retire somewhere else. He certainly wouldn't be hanging around Mildenheath any longer than he needed to. Mildenheath held too many bad memories for him. Southern Spain had always appealed, but the chance of bumping into Helen was too much to want to risk. It would, however, increase his chances of finding Emily. He'd always been conflicted about tracing his daughter, not wanting to upset her life as it was now. She was at an age where everything was volatile. Besides which, every passing day made it harder and harder to justify not finding her sooner. He knew he had the resources at his disposal to find her, and she'd know that too. He'd had no excuse other than his own pathetic sense of self-pity. Deep down, though, he'd always suspected he'd be a terrible father and that Emily would be better off without him.

Wherever he was going to go, it needed a beach. He hated beaches — never liked getting covered in sand and paying for sun beds — but having one nearby was vital. It was a psychological thing. Good weather all year round would be a winner, too. He'd always fancied Florida or the Caribbean. He and Helen had talked about going on holiday there, once upon a time. Well, Helen had, anyway. He'd been keen, but work had got in the way just as it always had. Right now, though, the thought of sitting under a palm tree with a glass of rum was extremely tempting.

All of a sudden, the thought of giving up and admitting

defeat had a certain appeal.

## 37

Wendy had been at Ambassador Court not so long ago. It was where Keira Quinn, one of the victims of the Milden-heath Ripper had lived. The flats were the cheapest possible private rentals in Mildenheath, starting at around £350 a month for a one-bedroom flat and, unfortunately, the relative deprivation and high number of re-homed ex-offenders meant that Ambassador Court was somewhere the police tended to visit quite a lot as it was home to quite a high level of crime.

Kyle Finney was one such resident, living at flat number 52a, which Wendy and Frank were standing outside, having knocked on the door twice. As they knocked on the door a third time, the door to the next flat opened and a woman in her forties came out.

'If you're looking for Kyle, he ain't here,' she said. 'He did a runner a few days back.'

'What do you mean he did a runner?' Wendy asked, concerned, as she showed the woman her identity badge.

'I mean he did a runner,' the woman replied. 'I come up the stairs one afternoon, probably last Wednesday it was 'cos I'd got my shopping with me, and Kyle was there coming out with two massive holdalls. I asked him where he was off to and he said he had to go.'

Wednesday, Wendy thought. Barely days before the deaths of Jeff Brelsford and Terry Kendall.

'Did he say where he was going?' Frank asked.

'Nope, didn't ask. But he seemed agitated. Said something about needing to get away.'

Wendy and Frank exchanged glances.

'How well do you know Kyle Finney?' Wendy asked.

The woman put her hands on her hips. 'Not all that well. I mean, we lived next door to each other but that don't mean nothing nowadays does it? All sorts of people coming and going in these places. I'd wager most people probably don't have a clue who their neighbours are.'

Wendy simply smiled. She didn't want to be the one to have to break it to this woman that she'd been living next door to a convicted sex offender. 'How long had you both been living here?' she asked.

The woman curled her bottom lip as if she was thinking hard. 'I've been here about three years now. Three years next month. He was probably only there a few

months, though. Don't know the date. You'd have to speak
to the housing association. Think they were putting
him up.'

'Has anybody been to the flat since he left?' Wendy
asked. 'No noises, anything like that?'

'Nope, nothing,' the woman replied. 'Takes the bloody
housing association ages to do anything. There's people out
there crying out for a home and they've got places like that
sat empty for months on end sometimes. You'd think they'd
pull their bloody fingers out wouldn't you?'

Wendy couldn't help but agree. She'd seen time and
time again the trouble that was caused in people's lives by
simply being unable to get a roof over their heads. With a
little more action in turning round abandoned properties,
they could solve a large proportion of the problem fairly
quickly and easily.

She gave the woman her card. 'If you hear anything or
think you might know where he is, can you give me a call?'

The woman studied the card intently. 'DS? That's a
detective, ain't it? Blimey. What's this all about?'

'I'm afraid we can't really say,' Wendy replied. 'It's part
of an ongoing investigation. But if you hear anything,
please give me a call.'

Back down at ground level, Wendy phoned into the
control room to have an alert put out on Kyle Finney. She'd
requested that all officers be on the lookout for him and

that if spotted he should be detained and brought into Mildenheath for questioning.

'You go back,' she said to Frank. 'I've got something I need to do. I'll see you back there.'

38

Wendy was trying to concentrate on the job in hand, but one infuriating thought kept flooding back into her mind. She knew Jack had been unreasonable. There was nothing new there. But even being as stubborn as he was, he'd never gone as far as he had this time. Before, there'd always been a sense that despite his stubbornness and complete unwillingness to see things from other people's points of view, he might just have been right. This time, though, it was different.

The amount he was drinking and the pit of despair he'd fallen into had meant that she couldn't predict how he was going to react. Of course, she knew Culverhouse probably wouldn't react brilliantly if she told him she suspected he might have something to do with the deaths of two sex offenders in the town, but she suspected the old Jack

Culverhouse would have either laughed it off or told her she was being stupid. Instead, he'd got angry.

She might well be jumping to conclusions. She knew that much. She wasn't even sure whether logic was telling her Jack could be involved or he couldn't possibly be. She couldn't tell heart from head any more.

The basic facts, as she could tell, were that Jack Culverhouse had inexplicably looked up a list of sex offenders in the local area without any operational reason to do so. Not long after, two of the people on the list were murdered by the same person. The killers used a taser to stun the victims before they were killed — a weapon which, she presumed, Jack Culverhouse would have the contacts to source.

There'd been no flag that Jack Culverhouse's DNA had been found at the scene of either of the killings, but then why would it? The DNA of serving police officers was kept on file in the UK and, in the case of Jeff Brelsford, Jack *had* been at the scene as the senior investigating officer. As for Terry Kendall's killing, well, he could just have been careful, couldn't he? No. She told herself she was being stupid. If Jack had killed Terry Kendall, he'd have been even more careless considering the mental state he was in.

It just didn't add up. But then again, his complete conviction that whoever was killing these people was some sort of hero had been extremely disturbing. Not surprising, but disturbing.

She really didn't know what to think, but she knew she couldn't rule out any possibilities. One of the first rules of good policing, though, was to never presume anything. As far as the operation was concerned, she knew the most professional thing to do was to investigate her concerns but not let them rule her. After all, right now she needed Jack Culverhouse.

He looked genuinely surprised to see her as he opened his front door and stood aside to let her in.

'Come to arrest me, have you?' he said, in a sarcastic, flippant tone.

'No. I've come because I need your help.'

Culverhouse made a noise of derision and closed the door behind him as Wendy made her way into his kitchen. The sink was piled high with dirty dishes. At least they weren't still sat around the living room, she thought.

'Fucking cheek you've got coming here asking for help. What am I, a cold-blooded killer or some sort of guardian angel? Give me a clue, will you?'

Wendy swallowed and looked at the floor.

'I'm sorry, alright? Look, this case is really getting to me. It's not an easy one to have to get my head round, all things considered.'

Culverhouse said nothing.

'Jack, I said I'm sorry. We need to investigate all possibilities and all leads, you know that.'

'And what bloody leads have you got that suggest I had something to do with this exactly?' he asked, folding his arms.

'We've been through this. And I've said sorry. I didn't think you did have anything to do with it. Not really. I just... Look, we all do stupid things. Can we just put it behind us?'

Wendy could see the sides of his jaw moving as he clenched his teeth.

'I think it might take a bit more than that,' he replied, finally.

'Fine. Can we start with a cup of tea?'

'No teabags.'

'Probably just as well,' she said, looking at the state of the kitchen.

He let out an involuntary laugh. 'You caught me just before my cleaning day, mum.'

Wendy smiled. 'Don't worry, I know the feeling.'

'So go on,' he said, after a few seconds of silence. 'What is it you want to ask me?'

Wendy took a deep breath. 'Kyle Finney.'

'What about him?' Culverhouse asked, his face neutral.

'You had some dealings with him, didn't you?'

'If by "dealings" you mean nabbed him for touching up

kids in the park, yeah. He got a three year sentence, served a year and a half and is out now. Why? Has he been done in too?'

Wendy, not for the first time, marvelled at Culverhouse's turns of phrase. 'No, he hasn't. In fact, he's currently our prime suspect.'

Culverhouse's face stayed impassive for a couple of seconds before he broke out into laughter.

'Prime suspect? Are you having a fucking laugh? What on earth led you down that road?'

Wendy shook her head. 'You know I can't tell you that, Jack. Operational sensitivities.'

'Yeah, and it was my fucking operation before Malcolm bloody Pope stuck his oar in. Was it him who came up with the idea that Kyle Finney did it?'

'No,' Wendy said, before thinking. 'It was Frank.'

'Frank?'

Wendy silently castigated herself for saying anything. She knew she had to tell him everything now, else the first thing he'd do would be to get in touch with Frank. Then it'd be out in the open that she'd discussed an ongoing murder case with a suspended officer.

'Jack, you have to promise not to say a word to anyone. This is serious.'

'Christ almighty, Knight. You don't need to give me the third degree on confidentiality. It might have escaped your memory, but I have been a police officer for quite a while.'

'I know,' Wendy said. 'Sorry. To cut a long story short, we found a van on CCTV that'd been seen near the scene of both murders at around the same time. The registration number took us to a van hire company in Birmingham who hadn't hired out that particular van but did have photos of it on their website, so it looks like our man might've used the photos to get an authentic registration and have false plates made up. We got onto the web host to find out who'd been on the site. There was one IP address from Mildenheath, not long before the killings started. We got onto the internet service provider and they confirmed the connection was made through Kyle Finney's router.'

'Just one question,' Culverhouse said, scratching his chin. 'What the fuck was a convicted child sex offender doing with an internet connection?'

'Christ knows. I should imagine it was extremely heavily monitored or restricted. I doubt looking at a van hire company's website would flag anything up.'

Wendy could almost see the cogs turning in Culverhouse's brain. 'It doesn't add up. I know Kyle Finney. He's a pervert, a dodgy fucker and a menace to society but he's not a killer. What would be the point? It's not like he'd see Jeff Brelsford and Terry Kendall as competition, is it? It doesn't work like that.'

Wendy tried to explain. 'No, I know, but—'

'Was the connection secured?' he interrupted.

'Sorry?'

'The router. Did he have a password or access code set up on it or was it wide open?'

'I don't know,' Wendy said, grabbing her mobile phone from her pocket. She called Frank Vine's number. 'Frank?' she said once he'd answered. 'Where are you?'

'I'm back at the station. Just got back a minute or two ago.'

'Right. Do us a favour and go back to Kyle Finney's flat, will you?'

'What? Are you having a laugh?' Frank said.

'No. Go up to his flat, get your phone out and see what wifi networks are showing up as available. Then give me a call back.'

'But I was just about to grab a quick—'

'Now, Frank!' Wendy said, her voice raised.

Frank mumbled something about his stomach digesting itself and hung up the phone.

'You've already been to his place?' Culverhouse asked her as she put her phone back in her pocket. 'So what are you doing here?'

'He wasn't there,' Wendy said. 'He's done a runner, according to the neighbour.'

'Really?' Culverhouse asked, raising his eyebrows. 'Interesting. Very interesting.'

## 39

Frank was starting to become seriously cheesed off with this job. He'd joined all those years ago to nab big-time criminals, not to trundle off backwards and forwards to paedophiles' flats to see how strong their wifi connection was.

The force had changed over the past few years, and that change had accelerated more recently with the guv being put on leave and pretty boy Malcolm Pope being put in charge of the team. Not that they'd seen hide nor hair of him, other than the odd time he felt he needed to come down and throw his weight around. Frank suspected Pope had bigger things up his sleeve. Probably too busy organising Mildenheath's closure and shipping everyone up to Milton House.

Frank wouldn't be going to Milton House if they moved. He'd told himself that much a long time ago. It wasn't his scene. The canteen was crap, the pubs were crap and the journey was crap. Steve Wing had suggested he put in for a transfer, but he wasn't keen. Any other force would be just the same now, centred around an office block and having more in common with an insurance company than a police force. They weren't even allowed to call it a police force any more; it was the police *service*. Load of bollocks that was, he thought.

No, he'd leave the police and do something entirely different instead. He'd always fancied helping out on the canals, moving boats and doing tours and excursions. He'd thought about setting up his own business doing it, but he didn't really know where to start. He'd find something. Anything was better than moving to Milton House. He wouldn't need much, anyway — statutory retirement wasn't all that many years off.

He pulled out of the secured car park at the station and headed off in the direction of Ambassador Court. It wasn't a great idea to go one-up to a place like Ambassador Court, and it certainly wasn't ideal to leave a police car unattended there, but he was buggered if he was going to walk it.

Barely five minutes later, he was parked up and puffing his way up the stairs to number 52a. When he got there, he pulled his mobile phone out of his pocket. It was a battered old iPhone, one of the early 3GS models. His nephews and nieces had been taking the piss and telling him he needed to upgrade. Apparently the model he had was nearly six years old. That was practically new, as far as he was concerned. It made calls, sent texts and allowed him to get some decent porn sites up, so what more did he want?

He went into his Settings screen, tapped Wi-Fi and waited to see what came up. There were hundreds of the buggers. He scrolled down, and one caught his eye. It was called *finney* and was showing as only one of two unsecured networks. He thought that seemed like a pretty good bet. Still unsure as to what this was all about, he phoned Wendy back.

'Yeah, I'm here,' he said. 'There's one that's named after his surname. Bit bloody stupid if you ask me, but get this — that's not the only stupid thing. He's left it totally open. No security. Just click and connect. Now, if you ask me, he should—'

Before Frank could finish speaking, Wendy had hung up the phone. Charming. Absolutely charming.

*Fucking job*, he thought as he puffed his way back down the steps.

## 40

'It was unsecured,' Wendy said. 'No security, according to Frank. And it's definitely his network. It's called Finney.'

'Doesn't surprise me,' Culverhouse replied. 'Kyle Finney is one sandwich short of a picnic, or whatever you're meant to call it these days. I quite like "mental retardation" but apparently the PC brigade don't.'

Wendy stood aghast at his comments. Even after all these years, she still found herself surprised every time he came out with a clanger like that. She thought people were supposed to mellow in their old age.

'But don't you see what this means?' Wendy asked.

'Well yeah,' Culverhouse replied. 'It means he's not got the brain cells to remember anything other than his own name. What a surprise.'

Wendy raised her voice, excited. 'No, it means anyone could have accessed his wireless network. And they would have known it was his, too. They could have been doing it deliberately to try and set him up.'

'Wait,' Culverhouse said, raising his hand. 'So is Kyle Finney meant to be a killer now or a potential victim? Because there's no way he's a killer, and if he's the victim then why would the killer want to draw attention to him? Surely he'd want the police staying well away so he could do what he had to do.'

'Perhaps it's just one big mistake,' Wendy said, after thinking for a few more seconds.

'How do you mean?'

'Well, say the killer's had his sights set on Kyle Finney as one of his targets for a little while. What if he's been sat outside the flat watching him? It's perfectly possible that he could've connected to the network, knowing it was unsecured, and used that access to monitor Kyle Finney's web traffic. He would've seen all of the websites he went on, potentially read his emails — who knows? If we're talking about someone who's pretty hot with computers, the sky would be his limit, surely?'

'You're asking the wrong bloke,' Culverhouse replied. 'So what, this computer genius just happened to accidentally browse the van hire company's website using Kyle Finney's wifi connection?'

'It's possible,' Wendy said. 'I've got a Mac laptop at home and an iPhone. Both made by Apple. If I connect to a wifi network on one, it saves the settings and the other device automatically connects when it's in range too. No need to re-enter the passcode or anything. What if our killer was connected to Kyle Finney's wifi network, thought he was being smart by searching the van hire company's website on his mobile but hadn't realised it had automatically connected to the same network?'

Culverhouse rubbed the untidy beard growth on his chin. 'It'd be a hell of a bollock to drop, but I suppose it's possible. You'd have to check that with the tech boys.'

'I think the first thing we need to do is find Kyle Finney,' she said. 'If he's not the brightest spark, as you say, then why would he be the only victim to have realised he was being targeted and manage to disappear?'

'Paranoia, probably,' Culverhouse said. 'He's probably not being targeted at all. I imagine he'll come back in a few days with his tail between his legs.'

Wendy grimaced and shook her head. 'No, I don't think so. This just doesn't quite seem right. We have to find him. Do you have any idea where he could've gone?'

'Me?' Culverhouse asked.

'Yeah, you've had dealings with him in the past.'

Culverhouse chuckled. 'Oh yeah, I've had dealings with him. And I know exactly where he will have gone.'

'Where?' Wendy asked, before realising how desperate she'd probably sounded.

'No. No way,' Culverhouse replied, leaning back and crossing his arms. 'Kyle Finney is a fucking menace to society. I've been waiting for someone to finish that bastard off for years. There's no way he should be out on the streets, living in civilised society.'

'Jack, his life could be in danger, he—'

'Good. Do you realise what he's like? He touches young girls up in the park, for Christ's sake, Knight. God knows how many times he's got away with it, but even the ones we've caught him for he's only ever got short sentences, then he gets out and does it all again. Nearly ten years ago I first nicked him for getting his knob out on the bus. Every time he gets back on the streets, he does something worse.'

Wendy stood open-mouthed. 'Do you realise what you're saying? If you know where Kyle Finney is, that's really fucking serious. You're perverting the course of justice. You're withholding information. You'll never work in the police force again.'

Culverhouse let out a deep belly laugh and shook his head. 'Do you really think I care? What have I got to lose? Look at me. I'm sat in week-old clothes, pouring scotch on my cornflakes. I've become what every good copper becomes. A husk. I'm never going back to work anyway. Not now Malcolm Pope's got his foot in the door. You know that and I know that. I'm not stupid.'

Wendy couldn't believe what she was hearing. She was watching him throw it all away before her very eyes. 'Jack, think about this. You'll lose everything.'

'Nothing to lose,' he said, staring at the ceiling. 'I don't need the pension. My reputation's shot as it is, and the new fucking bureaucrats will make sure that all my good work's forgotten as soon as I'm gone anyway, whatever happens.'

Wendy swallowed, trying not to let this affect her. It wasn't even the fact that he was obstructing her investigation that enraged her; it was watching this proud man, this officer who'd kept Mildenheath CID running for so many years, throw his entire career away in front of her.

'Jack, please think about this. Think long and hard. You've given your life to this, to seeking justice. You can't waste all that good work because of a couple of bastards.'

Culverhouse's jaw clenched and he turned to face Wendy.

'My mind's made up. You won't change it. The only person I'd ever reveal Kyle Finney's location to is the killer.'

41

Wendy had left Jack Culverhouse's place incredulous. He'd always been a stubborn bastard, but this time he'd crossed the line.

She knew she needed to get into Kyle Finney's flat and see if there was anything in there which could lead them to his location. The usual protocol would've been to go to the senior investigating officer for clearance, but she was in absolutely no mood to speak to Malcolm Pope. Anyway, he'd probably have wanted a written report, a meeting and God knows what other red tape before he'd give authorisation, at which point it could well be too late for Kyle Finney.

No, she only had one option: she had to go over Malcolm Pope's head. Fortunately for her, Chief Constable Charles Hawes was in good spirits as she volleyed off an explanation as quickly as she could, hoping that he'd sense her desperation and authorise a forced entry to Kyle Finney's flat. In her haste, though, she'd accidentally mentioned Culverhouse's lack of cooperation in the matter.

'What the fuck's Jack playing at?' Charles Hawes asked once she'd finished speaking. 'He could be strung up for this.'

'I know,' Wendy replied. 'He's hell bent on destroying himself. Quite frankly, though, he's not my priority right now. My priority is getting to Kyle Finney before the killer does.'

Hawes didn't need much persuading. Not long after, she was back at Kyle Finney's flat with a search team, including two burly-looking officers who had custody of a tool known as the Enforcer — a manual battering ram which could hit a door with more than three tonnes of pressure behind it. Wendy thought that would be more than enough for the rather flimsy-looking door on the front of Kyle Finney's flat, and she was right: it gave way after just one swing of the Enforcer.

With Frank Vine having decided against visiting the flat for the third time that day, Wendy entered the flat with Steve Wing and Debbie Weston, each of them splitting off to a different area of the flat to search for anything which might reveal Kyle Finney's location.

The flat was a mess, which to the untrained eye might seem more difficult to search than a tidy home, but the fact was that tidy people tidied away clues. Untidy people were more careless and prone to leaving clues lying about. All Wendy could see lying about, though, were pairs of dirty underpants and snotty tissues.

It amazed her how people could live like this. It was one thing not being a neat freak — she wasn't terribly house proud herself — but actively living amongst filth, germs and dirty pants was just another level altogether. Who wanted to sit in a pile of snotty tissues?

Having said that, the flat felt somewhat homely. Needless to say, she wouldn't have wanted it to be her home, but it certainly felt like it was *someone's* home. There was the usual assortment of bills on the side table — mobile phone, broadband internet, council tax. Behind them, propped up against a wall, was a photo of two young boys, clearly taken a fair few years earlier, sitting on a beach.

'Kyle and his brother,' Steve said. 'I remember the guv saying something about him when he nicked him last time. The brother died when he was about eleven. Cystic fibrosis. Really buggered Kyle up, apparently. Psychologists reckon that explains the way he is, but the guv tried to get it overturned. Said it was a load of bollocks.'

'Why doesn't that surprise me?' Wendy said, studying the photograph.

'I know. I think he went a bit far on that one, personally. They were clearly close as kids,' Steve said.

Wendy was surprised. She'd never heard Steve Wing think Culverhouse had been anything other than a god.

'That'd mess with anyone's head,' he continued. 'I remember being well upset when my gerbil died. I was only six.'

Wendy looked at Steve, her fleeting admiration for him suddenly vanquished. 'I'm not quite sure that's on the same level as losing your brother to a horrible disease,' she said.

'Well, no, but you know what I mean. I kind of know where he's coming from.'

'Right,' Wendy said, not trusting herself to say any more.

She looked around Kyle's flat and was surprised to discover that there was no TV in sight. She guessed that he probably didn't need one in this day and age, especially seeing as he was able to watch TV over the internet without having to pay for a TV licence.

It always amazed her how different people lived, and how no two people were the same. Before becoming a police officer she'd always assumed that 'homely' had a single definition, but she'd since come to realise that it actually meant very different things to different people.

'Sarge, come and look at this!' Debbie Weston's voice called from the bedroom. Wendy followed it.

When she reached the bedroom, she found Debbie sat on what she presumed was Kyle Finney's bed, holding a photo album which contained a few photographs, the rest of which were spread out over the bed.

'They all seem to be from the same place,' Debbie said. 'But taken at different times. Look, there are dates in the corner. Looks like some woods of some sort.'

'It is,' Wendy said, picking up one of the photos. 'It's Farnelsham. My dad used to take me when he wasn't working.'

Momentarily, Wendy was transported back to her own childhood, walking through the woods and down to the lake, a green, shimmering expanse of water surrounded by tall oak trees. It was a peaceful, tranquil place where she'd always felt safe. It was only about fifteen minutes outside Mildenheath by car — close enough to be perfectly accessible whenever they wanted to go but far enough that it felt like a temporary escape. Judging by the photographs in front of her now, it also held memories for Kyle Finney.

'They're all at the same place,' she said. 'These photos. They were all taken near the old boathouse.'

'You know it?' Debbie asked.

'Yeah. Yeah, you could say that,' Wendy replied, trying to hold back her own emotions.

## 42

The cold, damp brickwork felt reassuringly comforting against his back as he pulled the sleeping bag up over his legs. The sun was starting to disappear over the tops of the oak trees and it would be starting to get cold.

The ducks quacked merrily on the lake and he imagined they were quite happy with him being there. They always had been.

He'd told himself that he'd only be here for a couple more days. That was probably all he needed, and then he'd have to head out to buy more supplies. The food he'd crammed into his rucksack would only be enough to last him a little while, but he'd been sparing with it so it would last longer. After all, he wasn't exerting any energy out here. Just sitting, watching, thinking.

He knew the way he felt about things wasn't normal, but most of the time that didn't affect him. He had very few concerns in this world. Right now, those concerns were the two that had remained constant for so many years: this place and Petey. His bottom lip quivered as he thought back to the happy times they'd had. For a fleeting moment he swore he could hear Petey's cheeky laugh as they ran across the sodden leaves, chasing each other through the woods as their mother called after them to be careful.

Good times.

He felt a tear run down his cheek and he wiped it away with the back of his hand, sniffing as he did so. Bloody cold weather. It always did this to him. He didn't care. He was happy here. These were happy tears, he told himself. Nice memories. Memories were all he had now.

It was peaceful enough here during the day. There were a few dog walkers, but they didn't disturb him. Inside the old boat house, he was safe. He couldn't be seen by anyone and no-one would be doing what he and Petey used to do all those years ago: creating a raft from old driftwood they'd got from the seaside and tying it up at the edge of the lake. It was the only way across the water to the old boat house, which sat proud of the water on its own little island barely forty feet from the edges of the lake. Just far enough to be out of the way.

He looked over at the bright pink lilo, deflated and folded up in the corner of the boat house. It had been his only way to get to the boathouse in recent years, ever since that day he came back after Petey had died and found the driftwood raft gone. He didn't know whether someone had taken it, destroyed it or whether something far more special had happened. His Petey had been taken, and so had their raft. It seemed right somehow.

He pulled the sleeping bag up a bit further, nestled further into the cold brickwork and wiped another tear from his cheek.

## 43

It had been worth biding his time. Rushing in all gung-ho was never a great idea. He knew Kyle would come here and he knew at some point he'd have to leave. After a few days his defences would be down; he'd be cold, demoralised, fed-up. He'd start to think about leaving. That was when he'd strike, under cover of darkness. That was how an operation became a success.

The police had been doing their PR bit as far as Kyle was concerned, but that just wasn't good enough. Chuck him in jail for a few months and hope he'd be a changed man when he came out? Not bloody likely. As far as he was concerned, Kyle Finney was a mental case. And he'd only get worse.

The longer he left it, though, the more likely it was that someone was going to either spot him or come looking for

Kyle. That's why he knew he had to strike tonight. It was the sweet spot between waiting and over-waiting.

He looked out across the lake, his night-vision binoculars cold and heavy in his hands, the chilled metal eye rings bitter against his eyes. The heat source — or waste of oxygen, as he called it — was still there. He turned and looked at the camera strapped to the tree. It'd detect any movement from heat sources and send an alert to his mobile phone. So far, it had mostly picked up a couple of foxes and badgers, but Kyle would have to leave the boat house soon. He'd better hurry up, though, he thought; the batteries would only last another forty-eight hours or so. As quietly as he could, he made his way back to the van and waited.

## 44

Wendy, Steve and Debbie had got to Farnelsham in a little under ten minutes, beating the armed response unit they'd requested assist them. Wendy had asked them to hold back once they arrived and wait for further orders as she didn't want them to spook the killer if he should be there.

As the car pulled up, Debbie took a phone call. A few seconds later, she'd hung up and turned to Wendy.

'Armed response are minutes away, apparently,' Debbie said.

Steve snorted. 'I've heard that one before.'

Wendy told Steve and Debbie to quietly make their way round to the other side of the lake and keep an eye out. It would take them a good few minutes to get round there, and she knew that splitting up probably wasn't the best idea but it was better than leaving an area uncovered or waiting for back-up and risking Kyle Finney's life.

As she came into a clearing just before the lake, Wendy saw the white van parked up a little further round the lake between some large, thick bushes. She couldn't make out the registration number at that distance, but she didn't need to. She knew whoever was driving the van would've changed the plates again by now and she certainly didn't believe it was a coincidence that a van identical to the one seen near the scene of the two previous murders was now parked up a hundred yards or so away from where she suspected Kyle Finney was hiding.

She clenched her fists and muttered quietly to herself, willing the armed response unit to hurry up. She'd left her radio in her car and requested contact by text message only, not wanting to alert the killer with the sound of voices.

The woods and the lake were almost silent, save for the sound of the occasional owl hooting in the trees or a fox or badger scurrying through the undergrowth. It was then that she saw the figure of Kyle Finney emerge from the boathouse, carrying what looked like a lilo, glinting under the moonlight.

Her phone vibrated silently in her pocket. She pulled it out and masked the screen, stopping the light from casting any further, and read the message.

*At location. Making way to lake.*

They'd be a couple of minutes at the most, she reckoned. She looked up and saw Kyle paddling across the lake on the lilo. Fuck. He was heading to the other side of the lake. He could be ashore and gone by the time they got here.

She quickly tapped out a text message to Steve and her finger hovered over the send button as she noticed the signal indicator blank out, to be replaced by the words *No signal*. Fuck. She looked up again. Kyle was almost at the shore. She squinted and tried to look further into the trees on the other side of the wood to see if she could spot Steve or Debbie, but realised they probably hadn't made it round there yet. There was only one thing for it.

As quickly as she could, she started to sprint around the lake in the other direction to the one Steve and Debbie had gone in. With any luck, a pincer movement might work.

The leaves were soft underfoot, the recent rainfall meaning that her feet were almost silent on the ground — something she was immensely grateful for right now as she tried to concentrate on where her feet were landing, avoiding all manner of rocks and dips in the ground. As she came to another small clearing, she looked up in the direction of where Kyle had reached the shore. She wasn't far away now, but she could see that someone else was closer. Someone very familiar, who was pointing what looked like a Taser at Kyle.

## 45

Wendy didn't have time to think. Her instincts took over.

'Grundy!' she shouted, watching as the dark figure walking towards Kyle froze and slowly turned towards her. 'Don't do anything stupid, Robin. It's over.'

'Go away, Wendy,' he called calmly. 'I'm doing the world justice.'

'You think that's justice?' she replied, hearing her voice echo off the trees and the surface of the lake. 'It isn't for us to decide, Robin. That's for the courts.'

'Oh, the courts do fuck all! Call it rough justice. Call it what you like. But the fact is it's still justice. Because when it comes to *scum* like this,' Robin shouted, jabbing his finger towards Kyle's head, 'there's no justice other than complete extermination. You'll never change, will you, Kyle?'

Kyle said nothing, but stood calmly, seemingly resigned to his fate.

'Put the Taser down, Robin,' Wendy called. 'There are firearms officers on their way. You'll be surrounded within minutes and they won't let you out in one piece. You know that.'

'Then I'd better get a move on and get this done, hadn't I?' he said, stepping back and lifting his arm up in front of him, the Taser pointed back at Kyle Finney's chest.

Wendy calculated that Kyle would probably hit the ground within a second or so of Grundy pulling the trigger. After that, it would take only another couple of seconds for him to pull a knife and slit his throat. She was a good ten seconds' sprint away. There was no way she could save Kyle's life if she ran towards Grundy now.

Grundy lifted his head and prepared to fire.

Wendy watched helplessly as she saw what looked like a rock hurtle through the air and land with a sickening thud in the back of Grundy's head. Barely a second later, Kyle Finney let out a blood-curdling yelp and collapsed to the floor.

She was running towards him before she'd even realised what she was doing. As she got closer to the groaning heap that was Kyle Finney, she could see Robin Grundy laying motionless in the dirt, the blood beginning to pool around his head. Steve Wing came panting through the undergrowth, having only just caught up himself.

'What the hell happened?' Steve said, huffing and puffing as he spoke.

The voice came unexpectedly as the figure of Jack Culverhouse stepped out from the shadows. 'Not half as satisfying as if it had been Malcolm Pope, but it'll do.'

## 46

Wendy had held off from asking Culverhouse the obvious questions for as long as she could, but now she was fit to burst. It had been two days since the events at Farnelsham and their relaxed chat over a drink at the Prince Albert seemed like the ideal time to bring it up and clear the air.

'Guv, how did you know?' she asked, getting straight to the point.

'I didn't,' he replied. 'Not for certain. But I had a pretty good idea. Kyle had those photos out when we went round to nick him a couple of years back. Later on, he told the therapists about the boat house and how him and his brother had played there when they were younger. He was obsessed with the place. It was the only place he felt safe. I guessed that was probably where he'd gone to.'

'But how?' Wendy asked.

'How did I get there? Taxi. You think I was in any fucking fit state to drive? It all started to make sense after you came round and mentioned the ViSOR thing. After you left, I remembered exactly why I'd done the search that day. It was because Robin Grundy had asked me to. Once I realised what that meant, there was no fucking way I was going to let him get away with using me like that.'

Wendy swallowed, still not quite understanding. 'But you said you wanted to shake the hand of whoever was doing the killings. Why would you want to stop him?'

'He used me, Knight. Underhand tactics. He put my fucking job on the line to further his own agenda. And we both know what I think of pricks like that.'

Wendy knew exactly who he was referring to. 'When did you know it was Grundy?'

Culverhouse dropped his chin towards his chest. 'Deep down? Probably before it even happened. Subconsciously, I mean. None of it made sense until you mentioned Kyle Finney, though. I hadn't heard that name for a few months, but then I remembered where. Grundy asked about him, like it was some old familiar case he'd worked on. But then I realised he'd been long retired by then.'

Wendy wanted to change the subject. 'I'm not quite sure how many times you can come back from the brink like that,' she said. 'You're getting on a bit now.'

Culverhouse raised an eyebrow at her. 'Got to keep people on their toes.'

Wendy smiled. 'Having said that, though, the scotch doesn't seem to have affected your aim, which is always good. Not sure Robin Grundy would agree, though.'

He chuckled. 'How is he?'

'Not happy. Bloody great lump on the back of his head for a start. Probably thinking himself lucky he's not Kyle Finney, though. They're still trying to get the Taser prong out of his nipple.'

Culverhouse let out a guffaw. 'Not a total waste of time, then.'

Wendy waited for Culverhouse to stop chuckling. She had to ask. 'Guv, what happened with Grundy?'

Culverhouse clenched his jaw. 'How do you mean?'

'You know what I mean. The ViSOR details. How did Grundy get the information?'

Culverhouse took in a long, sharp breath. 'Like I said. He used me. I'm not going to go into details right now, Knight. Besides which, it's rude to ask things like that of your senior officers.'

Wendy blinked. 'You're back?'

'Of course I'm fucking back. Hawes is on the way out, isn't he? He didn't have much choice. Now he's reinstated me it'll be a fucking arseache for them to get rid of me after he's gone. Smart move, really.'

Now it was Wendy's turn to chuckle. 'Are you seriously telling me that the only reason you're glad to be back on the force is because it means you'll get one over on Malcolm Pope?'

Culverhouse smiled. 'Another drink?'

# GET MORE OF MY BOOKS FREE!

Thank you for reading *Rough Justice*. I hope it was as much fun for you as it was for me writing it.

**To say thank you, I'd like to give you some of my books and short stories for FREE. Read on to get yours...**

If you enjoyed the book, please do leave a review on Amazon. Reviews mean an awful lot to writers and they help us to find new readers more than almost anything else. It would be very much appreciated.

I love hearing from my readers, too, so please do feel free to get in touch with me. You can contact me via my website, on Twitter @adamcroft and you can 'like' my Facebook page at http://www.facebook.com/adamcroftbooks.

Last of all, but certainly not least, I'd like to let you know that members of my email club have access to FREE, exclusive books and short stories which aren't available anywhere else. There's a whole lot more, too, so please join the club (for free!) at https://www.adamcroft.net/vip-club

For more information, visit my website: adamcroft.net

**No clues. No time. One chance to expose a terrifying secret.**

DS Wendy Knight has endured both tragedy and pain in her short time with Mildenheath CID's murder squad. Her grizzled partner DCI Jack Culverhouse has seen it all. But neither of them is prepared for a case without a single lead.

A journalist with her finger on the pulse of Mildenheath's corrupt underbelly is beaten within an inch of her life. With a comatose victim and a defenseless child as the only witness, Knight & Culverhouse must reveal the horrifying truth before the ruthless killer comes back to finish the job.

*Turn the page to read the first chapter...*

# IN TOO DEEP
## CHAPTER 1

Tanya Henderson let the last drop of red wine fall from the glass onto her tongue, before stopping for a moment to consider whether or not she should open another bottle. It probably wouldn't be a good idea. She knew that a glass or two of wine — and no more — often helped her to think more clearly, to put all of her stresses to one side for a few hours and concentrate on the task in hand. And what a task it was.

Her job as an investigative journalist meant that she was used to having to deal with some real shits. It was her responsibility to dig down into the murkiest depths of criminality and corruption, exposing those people who used their money and their power to create more money and more power. In her time she'd uncovered some big scoops: a billionaire American computer software tycoon who'd been siphoning off money that was being put into a charity foundation and a married Premier League footballer who'd been sleeping his way around half of London and paying off the women to keep them quiet. It wasn't anything that had particularly surprised anyone who'd paid attention to the news stories when they came out: it was an unfortunate fact that most people just accepted this sort of stuff went on.

As much as she loved her job, Tanya got frustrated sometimes at the amount of work that had to go into each investigation, not to mention the depressingly short odds that meant most of them wouldn't end up in a story. More often than not, there just wasn't enough evidence to go on. If people were going to commit a major fraud, they tended to cover their tracks pretty well. But even so, Tanya Henderson was there, ready to pounce on any tiny loophole they managed to leave. It wasn't high turnover 'churn' journalism — she might only have a story published once every couple of years — but she knew that when she did it would make her some big money and give her the satisfaction of exposing some of society's biggest crooks.

And she knew the case she was working on right now could potentially blow a hole in the entire system of local government. It was something that had come to her attention as a local resident, but which she was planning to expose using her position at a national newspaper. The Inquirer didn't have the biggest circulation of all the national newspapers by a long shot, but it enjoyed a steady readership of around 50,000 a day — more when they broke a big story.

The story she was working on right now was going to have to function a little differently. Locally, she knew the story would be huge, but for a national scandal she was going to have to dig deeper and find other instances of the tentacles of corruption creeping into local government around the country.

A lot of journalists she knew tended to form teams, getting younger, less experienced journalists on board to help gather information, speak to witnesses and generally try to build a bank of evidence from which they could form a story. But for every time that had been successful, Tanya knew of at least five occasions where one of the juniors had majorly fucked up and blown the whole story before it had even begun. That wasn't something she ever wanted to risk. Slowly, slowly, catchy monkey.

Before she could decide whether or not to open another bottle of wine, her mobile phone began to vibrate next to her on the wooden desk. As the phone skidded gently across the surface, she looked down at the bright display. It was a withheld number. Nothing unusual in her line of work. She picked up the phone, swiped her finger across the screen and lifted it to her ear.

'Yep?' she said — her regular greeting. Giving nothing away as usual.

There was silence at the other end of the line. She gave it a few moments before speaking again.

'Hello?'

Tanya heard a light click, and then the phone went dead. She pulled the mobile away from her cheek and looked at the display. It had reverted back to her smartphone's home screen. She was used to getting some abusive phone calls every now and again — it went with the job, and was one of the reasons why she changed her number every few months — but she'd never had a silent call before. She hoped it would be the last, but made a mental note to give her mobile provider a call in the morning, just in case she needed to get her number changed again.

Sighing, she leaned back in her chair. Christ, the mountain of data seemed to be growing by the day. That was one of the downsides to keeping your work to yourself, she realised. Still, it was better than risking the alternative. As she'd come to learn, you couldn't trust anyone but yourself.

She considered calling it a night. It was already gone midnight and her brain was getting to the point where it wasn't going to be doing her much good to stay up any longer. But those files, the gigabytes of documents — deeds, agreements, financial records — all needed going through. It all needed going through. And the sooner it got done, the more likely she'd be to have her scoop.

Before she could decide what to do, she heard the faint

sound of her doorbell — a soft *bing-bong*, just loud enough for her to hear it from this side of the house but not too loud that it made her jump. When you've got your head stuck into investigating some of the biggest crooks in society, anything can make you jump.

She yawned, locked the screen on her computer, stood up and pushed her desk chair out behind her before making her way through to the hallway. She enjoyed living here. It wasn't a small house by anyone's standards — the kids had plenty of space and Tanya was very grateful to have her own home office — but it seemed a whole lot bigger and emptier when John, her husband, was away with work, as he was this weekend.

As she got to the front door, she could see the blurred figure behind the glass — big, burly, black. But then again, everyone looked that way when they were standing the other side of that front door. It was a trick of the light, the frosting on the glass. Backlit by the glowing orange streetlight at the end of the driveway, a five-year-old girl would look menacing from the other side of that door.

Sliding the brass chain across and unlocking the latch on the door, Tanya froze for a moment as it swung open and she registered what was in front of her.

A man — probably — dressed head to toe in black, except for a pair of piercing green eyes that looked at her from two of the holes in his balaclava. The first time she registered the crowbar was when it flashed it front of her eyes, the steel reflecting the light of the streetlamp just before she felt the impact on the side of her skull.

She felt instantly sick, an enormous wave of nausea rising from the pit of her stomach as her brain released a huge surge of adrenaline to deal with the trauma. She staggered to her side, crashing into the door and hearing it clatter against the wall. She felt another blow come down from above, this time on the back of her neck, just above her shoulder blades.

The dizziness grew, beginning to overwhelm her, and she felt her vision and hearing start to blur and cloud. In the moment before she lost consciousness, she could just about make out the soft, unfocused smudge of white and pink at the top of the stairs and the faint voice that faded away into the distance.

'Mum? Mummy?'

**Want to read on?**

**Visit   adamcroft.net/book/in-too-deep/   to grab your copy.**

## ACKNOWLEDGMENTS

I know some eagle-eyed readers will still be frothing at the mouth because of the chapter where Malcolm Pope appears and details the changes he plans to make to Mildenheath CID. I spent the good part of a day agonising over whether to use 'another think coming' or 'another thing coming', but ultimately decided in favour of the latter because of its evolutionary and increasingly common usage. The uninterrupted flow of reading must always be the writer's aim. If you disagree, tough. You can fight me for it.

I'd also like to add a small note regarding the usage of certain terms and opinions, particularly in this book, which deals with some very sensitive subjects. I tend to write chapters and scenes from the point of view of a particular character or set of characters, and the opinions and terminology tend to be theirs. Please don't assume I agree with them!

There are a number of people I must thank for their help in researching this book:

As always, ensuring the accuracy and credibility of the policing side of my books is very important. Of course, poetic and artistic licence has to be accounted for — sometimes in huge doses — but it would be impossible to even know where to begin without the ongoing help of David Parry, formerly of Leicestershire CID, who has been an invaluable sounding board over the past few years. I must also thank Bedfordshire Police and PC Matt Taylor in particular for allowing me to spend the day following him around, seeing what happens in the day of a frontline police officer and asking him all sorts of daft questions.

To Jo Clarke for her very helpful information — particularly on district nurses in this book. She's a vital source of information on anything medical and has helped me a number of times with research questions.

To Dave Whitelegg, one of the UK's foremost computer security experts, and who gave me a lot of his time and expertise in helping to ensure the online and dark web aspects of the book were credible and realistic.

To Tim Bishop and Amanda Trappes-Lomax from Bonallack & Bishop Solicitors the information on property and probate law.

I must also thank the people who helped me to understand what the real victims in this book must've gone through. I spoke to a number of victims of sexual harassment and assault, many of whom had extremely harrowing experiences of sexual abuse — and much worse — at the hands of relatives, parents and family friends. Writing a book has many difficult points, but hearing at first hand what those people went through can only be described as harrowing. Their honesty and bravery, though, was truly humbling and I cannot thank them enough for the time they gave me. Some, quite understandably, didn't want to be named in this book, but of those who did I must thank RosaKiana Rossi and Bobbi Parish for the eye-opening insights they gave me.

Thanks go to my fantastic team of beta readers — too many to mention by name now, but all hugely valued and appreciated — and also to my wife, who's the first person to see anything I write, and who diligently makes sure the very worst bits never see the light of day.

Last but not least, my biggest thanks go to the Apple store in Milton Keynes who booked my laptop in for repair at the end of September, forcing me to actually get off my backside and finish the first draft of this book before then.